also written radio plays and dramatized books for radio. She has won the Whitbread Award and the Friends of the Earth "Earthworm" Award. She says, "When I write I don't try to create new worlds, but to look at what is strange and magical about the world we think we know."

Books by the same author

Lord of the Dance
Storm-Voice
The Burning
The Spring on the Mountain
The Stones of the Moon
What is a Wall After All?

WATCHING

JUDY ALLEN

illustrations by John Lawrence

WALKER BOOKS
AND SUBSIDIARIES

LONDON • BOSTON • SYDNEY • AUCKLAND

*I would like to thank Caroline Royds for inviting me to turn
the six Animals at Risk stories into a novel; Martin Jenkins
for invaluable advice and information on animals and habitats;
and Joe Kennedy for sparing the time to talk to me about
wildlife film-making.*
J. A.

First published 2005 by Walker Books Ltd
87 Vauxhall Walk, London SE11 5HJ

2 4 6 8 10 9 7 5 3 1

Text © 2005 Judy Allen
Illustrations © 2005 John Lawrence

The right of Judy Allen and John Lawrence to be identified as author and
illustrator respectively of this work has been asserted by them in accordance
with the Copyright, Designs and Patents Act 1988

This book has been typeset in Gill Sans

Printed and bound in Great Britain by Cox & Wyman Ltd, Reading, Berkshire

British Library Cataloguing in Publication Data:
a catalogue record for this book
is available from the British Library

ISBN 1-84428-948-6

www.walkerbooks.co.uk

For Joshua

CHAPTER ONE

He was sitting in a slowly darkening room, in front of the computer. His face was lit by the pale blue glow from the screen, which was reflected as two points of light in his eyes. That was why he hadn't noticed that dusk was gathering outside, and hadn't thought to switch on a light.

When he had posted the advertisement on the wildlife website, he had wondered if there would be any replies at all. In the end there had been so many he'd lost count. He had spent most of the day going through them, trying to pick out four. An educational trust had offered modest funding for his project on condition that he took four film students with him as part of their work experience. So he had to choose, but it wasn't easy. He was used to working alone and he didn't really want any of them.

He had looked in vain for applications from

Chinese students, in the hope of at least working with compatriots, but it seemed that was not to be. However, his own English was good and he was glad he'd had the foresight to ask for Cantonese or English speakers only. There were no Cantonese speakers though, and he knew he'd have to endure hearing his Chinese name mangled.

This project was important to him. He was making a pilot film in the hope of getting serious funding – most likely from several different sources – to spend as long as it took to find and film animals that had been brought to the UK from other countries and had become naturalized. He was calling it *Alien Invaders*.

If the funding was generous enough, he hoped to film in other places as well; but he had chosen to start in the UK because it would make the story more unusual. People expected wildlife films to be set in the Amazon, or the heart of Africa, in the desert or in the Arctic, in extreme and dramatic settings – they expected exotic animals *and* exotic locations. They didn't expect to see exotic animals in the British Isles, which seemed so small and so tame. He hoped that the very unexpectedness of it would give his project the edge over others – because others were certain to be looking for financial support in all the same places.

He had already put together an outline of what he planned to shoot in the brief time he had, but at the back of his mind he knew he was hoping to find something more, something unexpected. First, though, he had to set up the expedition and get himself to England.

By the time he closed down the computer, he had sent five identical emails of acceptance and countless identical emails expressing regret and rejection.

He chose Jenny first. She had applied for the job of researcher. Her application was efficiently presented and also she lived in England and so could be expected to have useful local knowledge.

Next he chose Jake, who had ambitions to be a wildlife camera operator and had applied for the job of camera assistant. He put him on the list because he seemed realistic and had made it clear he expected to spend his time carrying spare kit and generally making himself useful. Also, he had heard of him from a good friend. Lao Meng had met Jake six years ago when he was only twelve and accompanying his American father on an expedition in China. He had spoken well of him, and a personal recommendation was always reassuring.

Then came Anya, from Hawaii, who hoped eventually to become a sound recordist. Again, she had been realistic, saying that she wasn't even sure he would want a sound person because she knew he could record sound on camera, which would be good enough for a pilot.

There was a definite pattern emerging. He was not

choosing people who flooded the screen with their achievements and abilities. He was choosing the ones who sounded as though they expected to work hard, if necessary at a very basic level.

That was why Hannah, from east Africa, got the job of trainee production assistant. She had as much enthusiasm for wildlife documentaries as any, but she was willing to drive, cook, put up tents – whatever it took.

And then, when he had his full complement, he spotted the application from Miguel. Miguel, from the Philippines, was at art school in America but was currently in London on an exchange with a UK student. His hope was to become a wildlife artist, and though he had no plans to work on documentaries, he was keen to have the chance to see and sketch animals he hadn't encountered before.

OK, Miguel, he thought, why not one more? Another male would balance things out, and Miguel made it clear he expected nothing, not even expenses. He just wanted to tag along.

So there it was. He was now a team leader and he knew he must accept the role with good grace.

CHAPTER TWO

Hannah was jogging along the lane that led back to the farmhouse where they were all staying. The filming was going well so far, but she hadn't realized how little exercise she'd get. A lot of the time she was either standing around or else sitting around. Sometimes, even when there was something she could have done, she found Lee had already done it himself.

He had told all five of them to call him Lee, although it wasn't his real name.

Hannah could understand that it was quicker for him to do things himself than explain them to her, and she didn't want to be a nuisance. But she was beginning to feel rather useless.

She jogged past banks of late primroses with beech woods behind them and fields on the other side of the lane. The path curved and then the farmhouse was ahead. Jenny was out at the front strapping luggage onto the roof of the Landrover, ready for the next location. There was nothing useless about Jenny. She was cool and professional, and such an efficient researcher that she had found all the locations before the rest of them arrived in the country.

Hannah walked in at the back door of the farmhouse just as Jake and Anya arrived at the front door, back from their project in south London. They had been surprised and delighted to be sent off on their own to Putney and Barnes to film ring-necked parakeets. They were elated but tired, so Miguel volunteered to return the hire car they'd used. Hannah offered to follow in the Landrover to bring him back again but Jenny said, "No, I'll go, you'll want to take a shower."

Still useless, thought Hannah, as she headed obediently for the stairs.

As soon as everyone was together again, Lee called a progress meeting in the small sitting room of the farmhouse. He set up the monitor so he could show everyone the footage that had been shot so far.

He was pleased with the way things were going. He didn't say so, he never did, any more than he ever got cross when things went badly, but they could tell.

They watched the parakeet footage first, crowding around the monitor, trying not to block each other. It was quite startling to see birds that belonged in India and sub-Saharan Africa in such an English setting. Jake had two or three good shots of them flying from tree to tree or shooting past high above, the sun flashing iridescent green from their backs and wings as they banked and turned.

Anya fretted about the traffic noise she hadn't always been able to avoid, but Lee said it made a dramatic impact – you don't expect to hear the shrieks of wild parakeets and the engines of London buses at the same time.

Next Lee showed his own footage of wild mink, including a mink chasing and killing a young rabbit.

"Mink have been established here for quite a long time," he said, "ever since they escaped from – or were released from – fur farms. They're usually unwelcome because they're efficient killers and they take a lot of waterfowl, but in this area they are useful because they control the rabbit population."

He switched off the monitor.

"Two in the can already," said Jenny, with satisfaction.

"It'd be good to find something really weird, though," said Jake. "Something no one else knows about."

"We have limited time," said Lee. "We need to concentrate on subjects we can be sure of finding."

"You could get your wish tomorrow, Jake," said Hannah.

"Oh, yeah," said Jake, "tomorrow is the great lake monster gig, right?"

Lee raised a hand in protest. "We should relax and wind down from today," he said. "Tomorrow is not here yet."

"OK," said Jake. "Can I ask you something?"

"If you wish."

"Why do you want us to call you Lee?"

"Because my own name does not sound well in a foreign accent."

"But why Lee? I mean, I know it's easy to pronounce, but it's not any part of your real name, is it?"

Lee looked at him thoughtfully.

Jake, feeling he might have been rather pushy, fidgeted.

"Come on," said Jenny sharply, "everyone should be doing an equipment check so we're ready to start off early tomorrow."

"It's all right," said Lee. "I will answer the question. Lee is the name of someone I once met, in the days before I knew I wanted to make wildlife films."

It was the first time he had really talked to them properly, and even Jenny sat quietly and listened.

TIGER
Lee's story

"I can tell you when I first wanted to film animals," said Lee, "but I cannot tell you when I first became interested in wild things because I cannot remember a time when I was not interested. My father worked as a guide, first of all leading groups of scientists, and later – as the world opened up – small parties of tourists. But also he would take me out on our own expeditions, just the two of us, as soon as I was old enough to walk. Later I began tracking animals by myself, learning about them without even realizing I was learning. Later still I, like my father, made my living by them. But the time I am thinking of…

I had been visiting relatives in south China, quite a way from my hometown. While I was there I wanted to explore the area, which was new to me. I went on foot and alone, carrying everything I needed on my back. I was hunting, but I wasn't hunting for anything in particular. I was hunting for anything of interest that came my way.

When you do not know an area, the best plan is always to stop at villages. This is not only to rest and pick up supplies, but also to be discreet, to sit quietly, to blend in until people cease to notice you and begin to talk freely in front of you. That is how you pick up gossip and rumour. And gossip and rumour will tell you what is around so that you can narrow your hunt down to the most likely places, the most interesting creatures.

This one time, though, I did not have to wait for the gossip and rumour, they came out to meet me. What was more, I discovered that I was a rumour myself.

Word had travelled ahead of me and my reputation had grown until no one who knew me would have recognized me from the description. It was said I was a brilliant hunter who travelled vast distances looking for exciting prey. It was also said that once I chose my quarry I had never ever failed to secure it.

Before I reached the village I was walking towards, two men came out to meet me. These were grown men, they didn't send a child as a messenger, they considered me too important.

They took me into a house. Other villagers came in too, and more waited outside, listening at the open door. The woman of the house was preparing food, all for me.

They asked me nothing. They told me about my impressive reputation, and then they gave me their news. "There is a tiger," said the first man. "Out beyond the rice fields, out beyond the swamp, somewhere in the oak wood near the river, there is a tiger."

"We would prefer to kill it ourselves," said the second man, "but we might fail, or worse, the tiger might kill us. So even though we know we will have to give you some of the profits, we would prefer you to do it for us."

I said nothing. Keep silent and you may seem wise. Speak and you may reveal that you are not.

My technique seemed to be effective because all the adults – apart from the woman preparing the food – were looking at me with awe. The babies and toddlers of course ignored me, but there was a boy – I heard them call him Lee – who stood to one side and frowned at me.

He saw me looking at him. "I don't see why you want to kill it," he said.

"Because," said the first man wearily, as if he had already explained this often, "if you eat the meat of a tiger you become as brave as a tiger yourself. Which is why it's a bad idea to poison it."

"Also," said the second man, "its skin can be sold for an enormous amount of money." He turned to me. "As a hunter," he said, "you will know that this must be kept secret. It's against the law to sell a tiger's skin."

The woman brought the dish of food and set it in front of me. I think she was Lee's mother. He stood in front of her as she turned away and asked, "Does eating tiger meat really make you brave?"

"I have told you," said the woman quietly, "you are as brave as you think you are. Eating a rose petal will make you brave if you believe it will."

The others ignored her and the first man rolled his eyes upwards as if she had spoken nonsense, which of course she had not.

When I had eaten I made ready to go. No one had touched my pack but I had seen them looking at the gun, wrapped and protected in soft leather, which lay across the top of it.

Several of them offered to come with me, to help dig a pit for the tiger to fall into or to carry the carcass home, but I refused.

"To find the tiger," I said, "I must travel quietly and alone."

Most of them walked with me to the edge of the village. There they stopped. "Good hunting," they said – all except Lee. "Bad hunting," said Lee. "I hope it gets away."

I gave him a stern, hunterly look, but he stood straight and stared right back at me.

I reached the edge of the oak wood, by the river, in

the early evening. I walked slowly, watching the ground, and soon I saw the pugmarks of a tiger in the damp earth of the riverbank. Not just a rumour, then.

I walked more cautiously.

After a while I came to a clearing. A deer lay there. It was quite dead and most of it had been eaten.

I unpacked some of my kit, as quietly as I could. Then I waited.

Suddenly there was a sound like a rug being shaken in the wind and a huge bird – a vulture – flopped down onto the deer and stabbed at it with its beak. Another followed.

But before the second vulture could start to eat, something burst out of the long grass at the edge of the trees and ran at the birds – a big, golden cat with markings so like the shadows of branches and grass stems that it had been invisible until it moved. It was a fine tiger, a male, fully grown but young.

The first vulture flapped clumsily into the air. The tiger cuffed the second, slower bird with its great paw. Then it got a firm grip on its prey with its jaws and dragged it steadily, fast, back under the shelter of the oak, where I suppose it had been resting.

It seemed unaware of me. I could hear it tearing at the meat and I knew I should try and get a shot; but the tree was in the way and I was nervous. I moved very cautiously, very gently, but the tiger's sharp ears caught the sound. It raised its head, showed its teeth in a silent snarl – and was gone.

I knew I'd made a foolish mistake. I had been too close for safety and badly placed for a shot. I knew I must be more careful.

I waited through the night. The tiger did not return. It had already eaten well – it had decided to abandon the remains of its prey. So at dawn I sought out the fresh trail and began to follow it.

It was two days before I saw the tiger again. It was some distance away, walking around a craggy outcrop below a small cliff.

I followed.

By the light of the evening sun, I watched it sharpening its claws on the bark of a tree, stretching its full length against the trunk. I got it in my sights, but at the last second, even though I'm sure it didn't hear me, didn't see me, it moved and spoiled my shot.

At dusk I watched it washing its golden, striped fur with great sweeps of its rough tongue.

I knew I couldn't take it then – the light was bad and the shadows made it hard to judge the distance.

That night I watched it stalk another deer, creeping so slowly through the undergrowth that sometimes it didn't seem to move at all for almost ten minutes.

It was as patient as I was.

I watched it make its leap. I watched the deer

spring away and the tiger catch at its hindquarters and miss. The deer ran. The tiger didn't chase it. All its power had gone into the first attack.

I knew it probably always missed more than it caught – but it didn't matter; it caught enough. It was sleek and well fed.

Next day, in the heat of the afternoon, I watched it drink from the river, fling itself into the water with a great splash, and swim strongly downstream, just for the cool pleasure of it.

That was when I got my first clear shot, as the water streamed off the tiger's head and its body moved just below the surface.

The tiger saw me. It clambered out of the water, a little way downriver, and shook like a dog, sending drops sparkling all around. That was when I got my second shot.

The tiger faced me.

I knew it was no man-eater. With its sharp teeth and strong bones I knew it lived on deer and wild pig. I was certain it wouldn't go for me. And I got the fine head and great chest right in my sights and took the third shot.

The tiger snarled to warn me not to come any closer, but it did not attempt to attack me. It turned its back rather scornfully and loped away and out of sight, in among the oak trees.

I lowered my camera and watched it go. I had taken three shots that I was sure would come out well, and I hadn't had to use the gun. It would have devastated me to have to fire on such a beautiful creature – but if it had come to my life or his...

Anyhow, I packed away my camera and rested for a while before beginning the trek back to the village.

On the way I had to think very carefully about what I was going to say. Somehow I didn't want to lie to those people, who had seemed so greedy but were really just poor; but I had no intention of telling them about the tiger. They might go after it themselves – or they might call on a different sort of hunter, a trophy hunter.

Someone must have been keeping a lookout because as I drew near most of the villagers came to meet me.

"Do you need us now to carry him?" said the man who had spoken first when I arrived.

"I'm sorry," I said, "not to bring the news you want, but I'm afraid there's nothing to carry."

"But there is a tiger out there?" said the second man.

A difficult moment. "I am the best tracker and the best hunter in the region," I said. "I have covered the whole area you spoke of. If there was a tiger, I would have seen him."

That was the truth, if not the whole truth.

"Do you mean you didn't see a tiger?" said the

second man.

I stared at him until he began to fidget.

"Are you trying to pick a fight with me?" I said.

"No," said the man quickly, perhaps remembering he had never eaten tiger meat in his life.

"You're very wise," I said. "I'll be on my way then."

The villagers took it well. They decided the tiger had only been a rumour after all, and they shrugged off their disappointment and returned to work.

But as I walked away the boy, Lee, followed me. When we were clear of the village he ran, overtook me, then halted, standing right in front of me. He knew. I could see it in his eyes. He knew, and he trusted me now. "There is a tiger, isn't there?" he said. "I know there is — but I'll never tell."

I looked at him, wondering what to say. I didn't want to burden him with such a big secret, but I wouldn't lie to him, not even obliquely as I had to the others. So I smiled. Then I winked. He nodded, satisfied, and ran back to the village. And I went on my way, picturing in my mind the tiger, out in some grassy clearing, beyond the rice fields, beyond the swamp, behind the oak wood, resting, safe, not knowing or caring that he had been captured on film.

But if I had had the kind of camera I use now and not just a still camera, think of the footage I would have — poor light and distance wouldn't have been the problem they were then. As it is, the moving pictures of that tiger are only in my memory and I can never share them.

He looked around at his quiet audience. "And sometimes I use Lee's name," he said. "Not just because it is simple and therefore useful, but because I remember him with great respect."

CHAPTER THREE

They were travelling light, but with six people, their own kit and all the equipment, the Landrover had to be loaded very carefully. When they'd finished and climbed in, it seemed extremely full, especially as Jake had his video camera beside him.

"I hired the most compact camping gear I could find," said Hannah, "but it's going to be a challenge finding space for it."

"Two vehicles would cost twice as much," said Jenny sternly.

"I know," said Hannah. "I do know the budget's tight."

"Sorry," said Jenny. "Do you want to drive? You know where the hire place is."

They managed to strap the camping gear onto the roof but the tent and its pole and pegs had to go on the floor under Lee and Anya's feet. The rolled sleeping mats were further back, on the floor under Jake and

Miguel's feet. The lightweight sleeping bags, borrowed from Jenny's brother and his friends, were squashed in with the other luggage. Miguel had the box of cooking equipment on his lap.

"It's not exactly going to be a luxurious campsite, is it?" said Anya as the Landrover moved off.

"It will be the most over-furnished site I have ever worked from," said Lee mildly. "If you are serious about a career in wildlife film-making you will have to be willing to sleep rough. Not always, perhaps, but often."

After an hour or so they stopped so that Lee could take over the driving from Hannah, and Anya asked how long the rest of the journey would take. Jenny was cautious. "It depends on the traffic," she said. "Plus we have to stop to pick up groceries."

"Where will they go?" Anya asked, twisting round to look in vain for some space.

"We will not need much," said Lee firmly. "We shall not have time for feasting, and if we run out of water someone can drive to the nearest supplier."

"We'll shop as near to the camping place as we can," said Jenny. "There's a really big village about twenty minutes from the lake. The lake's called Monk's Tarn, by the way. Monks used to fish there a few hundred years ago, but the monastery is long gone. It's big for a tarn, and it seems to have something very large living in it –

which is why it's on our list."

"You mean like the Loch Ness Monster in Scotland?" said Jake. "Or Ogopogo in Canada?"

Lee shook his head but said nothing.

"This one's only been seen in the last three years," said Jenny. "Not for decades like whatever-it-is in Loch Ness."

"How did it get there? Is the tarn linked to the ocean?"

"No," said Jenny. "It's land-locked."

"But how can we be sure it's an Alien Invader?" said Hannah. "It might be British through and through."

"Too big," said Jenny. "Too big for a pike and too big for a British eel. No one knows what it is or how it got there. There's never been a really clear sighting and there's never been a photograph or a video record."

"So how do we know it's there?" said Jake.

"Because signs of a sizeable predator in the water have been reported by several bird watchers and one or two fishermen – the kind of people used to observing things."

The landscape changed as they drove. Rolling grassland scattered with sheep gave way to hills and crags, with almost no houses to be seen. There was noticeably less traffic on the road.

Twice Miguel wanted to stop, once to photograph a kestrel hovering above the roadside and once, even more urgently, to try and get a shot of a red kite; but Lee drove on.

"We need to get there and set up," he said. "I am allowing us to take a big risk this time. It would be perfect to record and identify an animal that is a mystery, but we have little time. If we are not fortunate, and do not catch it on film, I shall regret this and wish we had chosen a subject as easy to find as the parakeets and the mink. Remember, we are not equipped with underwater cameras, so our chances are already limited. I am sorry about the kite, Miguel."

"It's OK," said Miguel. "Maybe another time."

Any hopes of stopping for lunch were pushed aside by Lee's sense of urgency, and when they reached the large village Jenny had spoken of he parked outside a newsagents and everyone set out on a brisk quest. Jenny had written a list and she swiftly tore it in three and handed out the scraps of paper, sending Jake to the bakery for rolls and bread, Anya to the greengrocers for fruit and tomatoes, and herself and Hannah to the grocery store.

"Be quick," said Lee, "and buy as little as possible."

Meanwhile Miguel was allowed to run to the pharmacy for more film for his still camera, and Lee himself paced up and down near the Landrover, hoping to keep an eye on it without looking conspicuous.

By the time everyone came back, though, there were two old men peering in at Jake's video camera. They kept glancing curiously at Lee, who was standing in the newsagent's doorway looking tense, exotic and distinctly out of place.

The men turned as the group approached and one of them said, "Are you the film crew there's been talk about? There was a lass from a film crew up here a while back, asking about Monk's Tarn."

"That will have been me," said Jenny.

"So you've come to track down our monster, have you?"

"Perhaps," said Lee, abandoning his attempt to avoid conversation.

"Need any extras?" chortled the second man, and he mimed grappling with some large invisible creature.

"The tarn's not today" said Jenny quickly, "Today we're going much further to look for – er – caper-caillies."

"Shame," said the first man. Then he went on seriously, "The tarn beast's been coming ashore and making a fat living off some sheep up there. Not too good for the local economy. Hoped you'd corner it and they could see what it is they're dealing with."

"Excuse us," said Jenny. "I don't mean to be rude – but we've got a long drive…"

The two men nodded, smiled and ambled off.

"I'm sorry, Lee," said Jenny. "I shouldn't have said we'd be filming."

"It would have been better not to," said Lee. "Onlookers would be a distraction to us and a disturbance to our subject."

"What's a capercaillie?" said Anya.

"A big bird – like a grouse. Lives in Scotland," said Jenny. "I don't know why I said that. I don't think there are any near here."

"So this lake monster," said Jake, as they all clambered into the Landrover, "this 'tarn beast' – it comes out of the water, right?"

"No," said Lee.

"Those old guys said it did."

"They were mistaken," said Lee. "This is not an amphibian."

"Does that mean you know what it is?"

"I have an idea," said Lee, getting into the driving seat. "Hannah, have you got the map? Sit beside me, please, and navigate."

Jake assumed Lee would say more once he'd manoeuvred out of the parking space and was driving away from the village, but he didn't.

When they'd driven in silence for a short while Jake said, "What then? What do you think the lake monster is?"

"We shall see," said Lee. "Or perhaps we shall not.

There is no point in speculating."

"We were talking about your story," said Anya, "after you went to bed last night. We liked it. Everyone thought you were going to shoot the tiger with a gun, not a camera."

"You might have had to," said Miguel.

"I might have," said Lee. "I am happy that I did not. Enough. I need to concentrate. Here they drive on the wrong side of the road."

"When I inspected the tarn," said Jenny, "I got permission to camp right beside it so we'll have a good view all the time."

"You are the most efficient person in the universe," said Jake. "It's breathtaking."

"I probably should have sorted that out," said Hannah.

"No problem," said Jenny. "It's done."

"You're going to wind up as PA to the boss of some multi-mega corporation," said Jake cheerfully.

Jenny looked at him in horror. "Never!" she said. "I want to work with wildlife – on documentaries if possible."

Jake held his hands up. "OK, OK," he said. "I didn't mean to upset you. I just thought organizing was your thing, not animals."

"No, it isn't, it's wildlife. It's important to get things fixed up and arranged so you don't waste time.

I like getting organized, I like pinning things down and I think I'm good at it. But animals are far more interesting than any of that — animals do their own thing; animals surprise you all the time."

"Right," said Jake. "Sorry — I got you wrong. So what started you off, what got you hooked?"

"I can tell you that," said Jenny. "I can remember it really clearly."

SEAL
Jenny's story

"The first time I had a really strong feeling for a wild animal," said Jenny, "it was so strong I almost felt it was mine, even though I knew it wasn't, and never could be.

I was on holiday in Greece with my parents and my big brother Joe. It was all very beautiful and mostly I was enjoying myself, but my family were getting on my nerves.

They told me things, all the time. They were usually interesting things, but I got really fed up with the way they always knew stuff I didn't. They told me stories from Greek myths and legends; every time we saw a ruined temple or a broken statue they explained how it would have looked before it was damaged; they showed me how olives and lemons grow; they taught me how to eat an artichoke, and how to recognize a swallowtail butterfly, a spider crab, a stinging jellyfish. I can't think of anything they didn't tell me.

I remember sitting outside a café on the beach eating honey cakes and thinking that my head was so full it didn't have room for a single extra piece of information.

Then my father said he'd like us to visit a tiny rocky island we could see from where we were sitting. He said, "We must get a caique to take us out there," and then he just *had* to add, "Jenny, a caique is a kind of boat."

I put my hands over my ears and said I didn't want any of them to tell me a single thing more.

My mother said I shouldn't mind them all knowing more than me, it was just because they were all older. But that didn't help because I knew they'd always be older; I felt I'd never catch up.

Later we went down to the edge of the water, where the boats were moored, and my father talked with two of the fishermen. There was an older one who only spoke Greek, but he had a son, Stefanos, who spoke good English.

He was really nice, Stefanos, very friendly and helpful, but when my father asked about a trip to the island he shook his head and said it was only a rock and no one went there.

My mother said we'd like to have a picnic on it, but Stefanos said it wasn't possible. He said there were a lot of submerged rocks around it, which would tear the bottom out of his boat. But to make up for it he offered to take us night fishing.

He took us out at sunset, and it was beautiful. The sea was already dark coloured but the sun was still making a red path across it and the first stars were beginning to show.

The boat had big lamps fixed to the prow and when Stefanos lit them they made a soft hissing sound. Of course Joe had to tell me they were gas lamps and that was why they made that noise. I ignored him. But then Stefanos said, "They are called pyrofania. That means fire crowns," and that didn't annoy me. I didn't mind Stefanos telling me things, and I liked the name.

His boat had an engine but he didn't use it, he used the oars. My mother was watching the land, where thousands of tiny fireflies were flickering among the trees. But I was looking in the other direction because I'd seen something amazing – a silver seal.

My father said he wasn't sure if there were seals in Greece and my mother said there definitely wouldn't be silver ones. I think Joe believed me, but by the time he looked where I was pointing, it had gone – and even I was beginning to wonder if I'd imagined it.

Stefanos didn't say anything. He stopped rowing and lowered a net into the water, saying that we might get fish there. He said they came to the light.

And then I saw it again – pearly white, moving towards us and trailing shimmering streaks through the water. It looked completely magical.

I stood up to point to it and the boat rocked.

Joe shouted out that I was right, it was a seal.

The seal submerged again and my father explained to us that it wasn't really silver; it was just that there was phosphorescence; in the water. I expect he told us all about the microscopic sea creatures that form phosphorescence, but I didn't listen. I just wanted to know where my seal had gone.

Stefanos said, "They are rare and shy. I think it will go far away."

Joe said, "Well spotted, Jen."

After that I couldn't pay attention to anything else – I think they caught some whitebait that night and a small octopus – I just stared and stared at the sea until Stefanos rowed us back to shore again. But there was no sign of the seal.

When I saw it next day it didn't look silver any more, it looked brown. It was a long way out, and I stood at the edge of the sea near Stefanos and his father, who were sorting their nets, and watched it through my mother's binoculars.

Joe tried to get me interested in a row of octopuses hanging out to dry in the sun, but I ignored him and he wandered off. It was a bit mean of me, but I grumbled to Stefanos that Joe and my parents were always telling me things.

Stefanos understood. I think maybe his father was

like that with him. He said he'd give me something to tell them. He said I could tell them my seal was a monk seal.

His father said something to him in Greek. He sounded cross. Stefanos translated for me. He said his father was angry because he thought the seals took all the fish. Stefanos said it was the big fishing boats that took most of the fish.

The old man grumbled about something else.

"He says the seals get caught in the nets and tear them," said Stefanos. "That is true, but it doesn't happen often."

I asked if the seals escaped from the nets and Stefanos said sometimes they did, but sometimes not – and if they couldn't get free they drowned.

Later on I got a fright because my seal dived and didn't come up again – and of course I pictured him struggling in a net. But Stefanos told me that seals stay underwater a long time.

It seemed to me he'd been gone for longer than a long time, but Stefanos promised me there were no nets so far out and the seal would be fine.

Then, when we were back at the café – I think we must have been eating lunch or something – we saw a holiday yacht moor near the little rocky island and then a rowing boat was lowered and people went ashore.

My father was really fed up, and as soon as we'd

finished eating he marched off to Stefanos to say that if he wouldn't take us out there, we'd hire someone else.

Stefanos looked unhappy but he said, "If you must go, I take you."

We went next day, when there was no one else out there. We went in the morning, with a picnic and a bundle of beach towels. The little rock island was further away than we'd realized, and this time Stefanos used the engine; but he shut it off before we got to the beach and dropped anchor, saying he couldn't go any closer.

I remember I looked over the side of the boat and I could see dark rocks on the sea bed with tiny fish swimming among them.

My father said that the other boat had managed, but Stefanos just said they must have known a special safe route.

It seemed really unlikely that Stefanos couldn't find a safe route, if other people could, but he wouldn't be moved, so we had to wade ashore. It was hot and the water wasn't all that deep, so it was fun. My father gave me a piggyback, Joe balanced the picnic bag on his head and my mother carried the towels high.

Stefanos told us he and the boat would stay nearby. He said, "Any time you like, I will take you away from this barren rock to a beautiful beach I know."

My father said, "He really doesn't like people coming here, does he? I can't imagine why."

He found a flat rock to lie on while his shorts dried. My mother found a pool full of sea anemones. Joe found two small caves, which opened onto the strip of beach where we'd come ashore. The sun shone through a hole in the roof of one, but the other was shady enough to keep the picnic cool.

Stefanos rowed a little way off and lowered baskets, I think to catch squid. I climbed up to the top of the rock island to look for my seal. A bit later Joe climbed up after me to bring me bread and goat's cheese, a huge tomato and some cherries. Then he went back down again – so I was by myself when the seal's head appeared out of the sea below me. It was really sudden and it made me jump.

It looked straight at me and then dived. This time I had a good view; but though I stared for so long the tomato pips dribbled all down my front, it didn't come up again. I knew it must have gone into a cave under the island.

I crawled right to the edge and looked over. I could see Stefanos in his boat, but I couldn't tell if he was looking at me. My family were too busy eating to look up. I lay on my stomach and stared down – and a sleek seal head popped out of the water below me. For a moment I was only a couple of feet away from its face, then the seal somersaulted and sent up a flurry of sandy water. When the sand settled, the seal was gone.

So then I knew it definitely had a cave with an underwater opening. But there was no way I was going to dive down to find it. But I thought about the cave Joe had found, the one that opened onto the beach. That one had a hole in the roof, and I wondered if the seal cave might have one as well.

And it did. I searched around and I found the opening, half hidden by a little scrubby bush.

At first when I looked in all I could see was a pattern of shimmering green and gold all over the cave walls. Then I could make out a big cavern with a stony floor and rock shelves. The sun was shining through the sea and in at the underwater opening, lighting everything with a watery, shimmery glow.

And I was there, looking in, when the seal swam in through the opening and hauled himself out of the water and onto the little beach inside the cave. It was only then that I noticed three more seals lying on rock shelves, high up where I guess the sea didn't reach. Two of them had babies.

I could hear the sea making a soft sighing noise, and I could hear little bleating sounds from the pups. It was the most magical and beautiful thing I'd ever seen. I just stayed there, watching, for what seemed like a hundred years – and then, suddenly, I realized that for once in my life I knew something that not one of the rest of my family knew.

I stood up, but before I could call to them I saw that Stefanos was bringing his boat closer, waving at us and shouting that there was a storm coming and he had to get his boat back into harbour.

In the rush to get off the island I didn't have time to say anything. Joe piggybacked me out first and then waded back to help the others carry our stuff.

Clouds came over the sun and I could feel the wind getting stronger. But Stefanos kept the boat steady while we waited for the others to join us. Then he said that he knew what I'd found. He told me it was the last hiding place of that seal family. He said that if they were disturbed the mothers might abandon their pups, or even kill them. That was why he tried to stop people going there.

It was a horrible moment. I said I hadn't disturbed the seals, I knew I hadn't. Stefanos said, "No, I'm sure you didn't. But will you betray them?" And he glanced at my parents and Joe, packing up on the beach.

I said my family wouldn't hurt them – but Stefanos said, "They would want to look, wouldn't they? They would dive down, just once, thinking there could be no harm in that. And later others might hear them talking about what they had seen and come out to see for themselves."

I watched my family wading slowly towards us. I wanted so badly to tell them that it almost hurt.

Stefanos understood. "I give you something else to tell instead," he said. "Listen, hundreds of years ago people believed that a tent made of sealskin would protect them from lightning."

It didn't seem enough.

"And," he said, "they believed that if they dragged the skin of a seal round a field the crops would not be damaged by hailstones."

The bad weather had come so suddenly – the sky was dark, the rain was starting, and the wind was blowing my hair over my face. I could imagine there might be lightning and hail any minute.

Stefanos fixed me with such a look. "Will you keep the secret?" he asked. "For the seals?" And then the others were climbing on board and he was helping them.

The water was already choppy and as we travelled back it got worse. We all sat quietly at first.

Then my father pointed and said, "Someone doesn't mind the bad weather."

There he was, my seal, his head just above the surface of the water not far behind us.

My mother said, "It's always alone, isn't it? You'd think there'd be a whole family of them, wouldn't you?"

It was almost unbearable. I said, "I can tell you something none of you know." Then I thought of the seals and their young and I told the story about the sealskin tent and the lightning.

My mother said that was extraordinary and my father wanted to know how I'd found it out, though he must have guessed it was from Stefanos.

They were all, Joe included, listening to me with interest. I honestly couldn't remember they'd ever done that before.

I said, "I can tell you something else too."

The seal sank below the surface and Stefanos watched me.

I sat up straight in that boat and I told the story about the sealskin and the hailstones. Then I said, "That's all."

And I didn't mind any more that I hadn't told them the exciting part. It was worth it, for the seals, and – if I'm honest – for the smile Stefanos gave me.

CHAPTER FOUR

"So are the seals still breeding there?" asked Anya as Lee swung the Landrover onto a narrow track and they bumped over its uneven surface.

Jenny shook her head. "I don't know," she said. "I've never been back."

"Not even to see Stefanos?" said Hannah.

"No, sorry, I didn't go back years later and marry Stefanos and settle in Greece. Is that the story you wanted?"

"It would have been nice," said Hannah.

"But it was an OK story as it was," said Anya, then "Ouch!" as Lee brought the Landrover to a jolting halt. "Are we here?"

"We're definitely here," said Jake, "but is this the place?"

Lee said nothing, he just got out and stretched and then looked carefully around.

"Yes, this is the place," said Jenny, and one by one the rest of them climbed out, stiff after the drive.

There was a wood of towering conifers behind them. To the front the rough land sloped gradually down to the tarn, a wide expanse of water with a couple of tiny islets in it, neither of them more than half a metre across. To the far right a long low promontory, covered in scrubby grass, jutted out into the water. Beyond the tarn the rough, boulder-strewn moorland sloped away and gently upwards to a small rocky outcrop against the sky, which looked like a broken stone crown.

Each of the islets had a messy twig nest on it, one with a sitting moorhen. The sun, which had shone for most of the journey, was now covered by white cloud so the water was pale and bright, with a slight feathering of breeze moving over its surface. There were coots, moorhens and a few mallards scattered over the surface of the water.

Miguel raised his binoculars to his eyes in the hope of seeing something more interesting. "There could be other water fowl – or water animals," he said at last, pointing to the narrow promontory. "On the other side of that."

"How deep is the water?" said Jake.

Jenny looked at her notes. "About one and a half metres."

"That's not so very deep," said Miguel.

"Seems it's deep enough," said Jake.

"How would something big get in here in the first place?" said Anya.

No one offered an answer.

They made their camp on a flat piece of land between the track at the edge of the wood and the rim of the tarn. There was just one tent, with room for four sleeping mats; they would take turns to keep a twenty-four hour watch. There had been no reported night sightings of the tarn monster, but that was probably only because no one had been nearby after dark.

When the camp was organized they walked right around the tarn, noting the rocky edges in some places, the sloping muddy beaches or shelving banks in others. They searched for burrows or fissures under the banks, anywhere where a large water creature could lie hidden. They didn't find any, but they all knew that didn't necessarily mean there weren't any. In fact, although the tarn was not much more than sixty metres across, there were numerous possibilities for hiding places – in thick patches of weed, behind or beneath the little islets, or in the mud on the bottom.

"How are we ever going to see it if we don't go in underwater?" said Jake.

"All the reported signs and sightings have been from land," said Jenny.

"It hasn't been seen every day, though, by every person passing by, has it?" said Anya. "We're going to need a lot of luck."

But Lee said their chances were good. "Clearly it chooses to surface at times. Those who visit the tarn rarely, often alone and only for a few hours, usually to fish, have often been lucky. We are here for a solid block of at least forty-eight hours, with six pairs of eyes. We cannot all watch all the time, but we should be able to maintain four watchers constantly. I am hopeful."

As they walked back towards the tent, Jake said to Jenny, "I didn't see any marks or tracks where it had crawled out of the water."

"Lee said it doesn't come out."

"Yeah, but Lee doesn't know everything. He doesn't know this country at all – shouldn't we listen to what the locals said?"

"Bored old men passing on rumours," said Jenny.

"OK, I guess you're right." He raised his voice to call to Lee. "Where do you want me to set up, Lee?"

"I think," said Lee, "we will do best as six individuals. Use your instincts, all of you. But do not keep any sighting to yourselves, however small, however much you think you could have been mistaken."

Hannah went to the Landrover to fetch supplies to cook supper. "It's going to be gloop," she said. "There's only one pan so it'll all have to go in together."

Nobody seemed to mind.

The sun, invisible behind the pale cloud cover, was not yet ready to set, but the light was beginning to fade and the breeze was growing a little stronger, riffling the water right across the tarn. A pair of ducks was moving up on to the promontory, wagging the moisture off their tails, ready to settle for the night. Coots were giving their strange hooting calls and though one moorhen remained on her nest, the rest were scattered over the surface, still diving for food. Everything seemed peaceful.

When they were all sitting spooning up their gloop, in a row facing the water, Hannah said, conversationally, "I thought I heard an animal when I was in the wood just now."

"What were you doing in the wood?" said Jake.

"Oh, Jake, for goodness sake," said Jenny, quite sharply. "When you're camping, you don't ask someone why they went into the woods."

"Sorry," said Jake. "What kind of animal?"

"I didn't see anything," said Hannah, "I just heard it. I thought it might be a badger."

Jenny shook her head, swallowed a mouthful, and pointed with her spoon at her notes, which were on the ground beside her. "No badgers," she said. "I have a list of all wildlife sightings in the area, not just from the people who saw something in the lake, but from hill farmers and other locals. I have a list of mammals, reptiles, amphibians, fish and birds – I didn't ask about insects – but there are no badgers, not even any rabbits."

"Why did you do all that?" said Jake. "Still trying to find out stuff your family doesn't know?"

Jenny grinned back. "Oh, you should hear me telling them stuff now," she said. "No, I was just checking in case there was anything else we ought to try and pin down while we're here." She dug the spoon back into her bowl of gloop. "But there isn't," she said. "No exotics. But while I was checking I found that mice and voles are the largest mammals around here."

"It was a lot larger than a mouse or vole," said Hannah. "It sounded quite heavy – that's why I thought of a badger."

"Haven't you got the sheep-murdering tarn monster on the list?" said Jake. "Those old guys were locals, you know. We should listen to them as much as to anyone else."

"You're right,' said Jenny. "I wasn't taking them seriously and I should have. But I've remembered something – I know what they were talking about. There was a stray dog, a lurcher-type that had gone feral. It was seen worrying sheep."

"That must be what I heard then," said Hannah.

"No," said Jenny. "They shot it." She put the bowl and spoon down again and turned a few pages of her notes.

"Yes – they shot it more than two months ago now."

"Oh," said Hannah.

"It could have been the trees moving in the wind," said Miguel reassuringly. "When the branches touch they can make heavy sounds."

"No," said Hannah. "It was definitely something alive, and it was moving through the wood." She shrugged. "Oh well, whatever it was, I expect it'll mind its own business."

Anya looked back over her shoulder at the towering conifers that led away, over a floor thick with many seasons' worth of dropped cones and needles, until the trunks seemed to close in like a palisade, encircling darkness. "I hope so," she said, too quietly for anyone else to hear.

CHAPTER FIVE

At first they didn't notice the strangers walking slowly towards them.

The breeze had dropped. Even though there was no sun, shadows were deepening under the trees and around the rocks beyond the far shore of the tarn, as if night was seeping up from the depths of the earth.

In a break in the cloud cover, above the distant stone crown on the hill, the moon was visible. It was almost full, but pale because the sky was still light. As the air cooled, a thin mist was beginning to rise over the surface of the water.

No one was talking now. Everyone had pulled on sweaters.

Jake was setting up two cameras on tripods over on the neck of the promontory, the only place with a view of the entire water surface. Miguel was sitting cross-legged not far away from him, sketching the drifting ducks.

Hannah was at the campsite, clearing away after the meal, cleaning the pots and bowls with water from the tarn. Anya had unpacked her sound equipment and was kneeling beside the Landrover, checking the various microphones.

Lee was standing at the water's edge, looking through binoculars, scanning back and forth from shore to shore.

It was Jenny who noticed the walkers moving along the track at the edge of the wood. They were walking silently, and so close to the trees that they seemed to disappear among them and then reappear almost at once, a little closer. The combination of dusk and the silent, almost secretive, approach made her wary.

She walked across to the Landrover and stood in front of it, facing them to show them they had been seen.

They moved steadily on, and then the one in front raised a hand and waved. By now they were near enough for her to see a girl of about her own age, stooping slightly under the weight of an enormous backpack. She was followed by a tall young man with an even larger pack, using a long, broken branch as a walking stick.

As they walked up to her and stopped, the girl unhitched her backpack and let it fall behind her with a thump, and Jenny understood why they had been walking so slowly and silently, drifting in and out of the trees like ghosts – it was because they were both completely exhausted.

Their names were Katie and Ben, they told her. They were booked in at a campsite for the night, but they'd taken so many detours during the day to look at interesting things, that they were beginning to doubt if they'd have the energy to get there.

"Do you know how far it is from here?" said Katie, gazing pleadingly at Jenny, as if willing her to say it was really close.

Jenny made a face. "I'm sorry," she said. She knew the campsite the girl had named, it was at the edge of the village where she and the others had stopped to buy food. "It's quite a few miles, I'm afraid."

Ben sank down onto the ground and crouched on his haunches. "We'll be OK," he said. "If we just have a rest, we can go on."

Lee, first looking to see that Jake was still on watch over on the promontory, with Miguel nearby, moved over to join them. Hannah stopped clearing up and offered to make tea.

"We should keep going," said Katie. For the first time she looked around at the set-up, taking in the cameras and Anya kneeling by her recording equipment. Her eyes brightened. "Oh, you're filming!" she said.

"Just testing the cameras," said Lee quickly.

"We won't be starting for ages," said Jenny, equally swiftly, not wanting to repeat her earlier mistake.

Katie gave her a wide smile. "I understand," she said. "You don't want sightseers getting in the way and frightening away your quarry. We won't tell anyone we've seen you, I promise."

Lee relaxed. "Thank you," he said. "You do understand."

"So," said Ben, reluctantly heaving himself upright once more, "you're hoping to track down the big cat, are you?"

Lee just smiled, and Jenny shook her head.

"It's OK," he said. "I won't tell either."

"We're really not looking for any kind of cat," said Jenny.

"Fair enough," said Ben. "It's just – well, we've circled round this whole area, today and yesterday, and we keep hearing stories about a big cat that's killing sheep."

"Actually," said Katie, half-laughing, "one of the farm-workers way back there" – she gestured back the way they had come – "said it was a werewolf. But we decided not to take that too seriously."

"A werewolf!" said Anya, her eyes enormous.

"No, no," said Ben, "don't worry, the rumours are getting out of hand. The really weird thing is that one or two people seemed convinced the thing actually lives in the lake, which hardly sounds like a cat or a wolf."

"The last wolf in the UK was shot in Scotland in the seventeenth century," said Lee. "Nowadays, it would have to be a large dog."

"We only heard one werewolf theory," said Katie. "But whatever it is, it does seem to be something out of the ordinary. People who've lived in this area for generations are talking about it. They're saying maybe it's a puma or a lynx, escaped from a wildlife park somewhere."

"Lynx and puma can live wild in Britain I've heard," said Ben.

"They could," said Lee. "But most mysterious big cat stories are resolved when someone finds a feral dog..." He glanced at Jenny. "And then it is usually shot," he added.

"Dogs worry sheep," said Ben stubbornly, "but they don't usually eat them."

The low mist was beginning to drift beyond the edges of the tarn, towards the path. The sky was darkening and the moon growing clearer and brighter. Ben gave a slightly nervous laugh and nudged Katie. "Oh well," he said. "Whatever it is, at least it won't be hungry tonight."

"Why not?" said Hannah.

Anya was glad Hannah had asked the question; she thought her own voice might give away how she was feeling. She had discovered a whole new side to herself. Away from the places and people she knew, she was far more easily frightened than she had ever expected.

"It's already had a good feed," said Katie. "We stopped for lunch in a pub over the other side of the valley and there was a lot of talk in there. A farmer found a freshly killed sheep very early this morning."

"Its neck had been bitten right through," said Ben, "and it had been partly eaten. You can see where the werewolf idea came from." He shrugged. "I'm glad they're not saying it's a vampire. We didn't pack any garlic."

Lee pulled the keys to the Landrover out of his pocket. "I need a volunteer to drive these two to their campsite," he said.

"Oh no, we're OK," said Ben. But Katie cut through his words. "That would be brilliant," she said, looking as though she might cry with relief.

"This is not," said Lee, "because I think there is anything more dangerous than rumours out there, it is because you are both exhausted and a ten-mile walk is not sensible."

"I'll go," said Hannah. But Jenny said, "No, I will. You did the food."

"But you do everything," said Hannah. "All the research and finding the place, and half the driving.

I'm not earning my keep here."

"That's OK," said Jenny. "No one's paying our keep anyway. I'll go. I know the way."

As Lee went to join Jake and Miguel on the promontory, Anya nodded towards the departing Landrover and said to Hannah, "Those two must be what you heard in the wood."

Hannah watched the Landrover bumping off along the track and out of sight behind the trees.

"Can't have been," she said. "If it was, they'd have reached us sooner, however slowly they walked. Anyway, they came along the track beside the wood, not through it."

"Hey!" said Anya sharply. "Did you see that?"

"What?"

"Something dragged a coot down under the water. Over there. Near the middle." She ran out to the promontory, Hannah at her heels. "Did you see?" she panted. "Jake, did you get it on tape?"

Miguel was standing now. "I saw," he said. "But the light is so bad, it was hard to tell. I think perhaps it dived. Watch – see if it comes up again."

Lee was shaking his head in frustration. He had been looking where he was treading and not, at that crucial moment, at the water.

"I think I got it," said Jake. "Can't replay yet – got to keep watch."

"Right, I'm on my camera now," said Lee. "Wind back and check, Jake. The rest of you – keep watching."

The other coots and moorhens and ducks seemed undisturbed. Most of them had their heads turned right around onto their backs, ready for sleep. One pair of mallards had settled, probably where they always settled, in a patch of rough long grass only a metre or so away from them. There had been no sound, no squawk from the coot, no splash, nothing to disturb the other birds.

"They don't usually stay down as long as this…" Lee began.

Then, "Got it!" said Jake. He was rerunning the video, watching on the tiny viewing screen. Hannah, Anya and Miguel gathered round, and he ran it through again.

The coot had been some way from the camera. The dying light and slight camera shake as Jake moved to get the image in the centre of his lens had made the picture a little fuzzy, but it was clear enough. The bird did not give the usual little leap up before ducking its head and diving. It went straight down, as though something had pulled it underwater from below – and so swiftly that it didn't even have time to cry out.

CHAPTER SIX

It was dark when Jenny got back, but the last of the clouds had moved away and the moon was very bright. In its pale light everything was in shades of grey and black, but when she had switched off the headlights and her eyes had grown accustomed to working without them, she could see there was no one at the campsite. Looking across at the promontory she could see five figures. Jake and Lee both at their cameras, now working with night vision lenses, and the other three sitting together close by.

After what they had seen, no one wanted to stop watching and take a break, even though Lee said that now that it – whatever it was – had eaten, it would probably be quiet for a while.

"Anya's been telling us these werewolf stories," said Jake as he showed Jenny the footage of the coot's last moments. "Thanks for leaving me and Miguel alone over here without warning us!"

"Stories are not dangerous," said Lee.

"But they don't start for no reason," said Anya.

"You are not going to make wildlife films," said Lee, "any of you, if you are so easily frightened." He held up his hand, in his characteristic gesture, to stop their protests. "You will need to be willing to go to places where you are in real danger, not imagined danger."

"Yeah," said Jake, "but when people know there's real danger, they usually carry a gun."

"Go back to the camp," said Lee quietly, "all of you, and get some rest. I would like you to settle down and remember that you plan to become professionals. I will call you when I need you."

No one wanted to stop watching the lake, but no one even considered arguing with Lee.

They trooped back the short distance to the tent and hovered near the opening, no one really wanting to go inside and risk missing something.

"Why don't we sit and watch from here?" said Hannah in a whisper. "I don't think Lee cares if we rest, really. I think he was just sick of having us around him. If we stay out of his way it'll be OK. Does everyone agree?"

Everyone agreed.

They sat not far from the water's edge, still and silent. Most of the tarn was visible from there; only the stretch behind the promontory was out of sight. They watched the water, but they also watched the lone figure on the promontory, hoping for a sign if something happened they couldn't see.

But nothing happened, except that time passed. It was a while before any of them would admit it, but first they got rather cold – then, one after the other, they got cramp. Insects fussed around them. No one liked to flap at them in case they distracted Lee, so eventually the insects began to settle and sometimes to bite. But the major problem was boredom.

"It's got to be OK to talk," hissed Jake. "If we keep our voices down."

"I don't know," muttered Jenny. "Voices might annoy him."

"He's right over there." said Jake. "And we can talk quietly. Why doesn't someone else tell why they're here, what got them hooked? Someone else must have a story."

There was a silence. Then Hannah whispered, "I've got a story, but it's not very scientific. It's about a dream – and a necklace."

"Go for it," said Jake.

ELEPHANT
Hannah's story

"I saw the necklace for the first time when I was about eleven or twelve," said Hannah. "My mother pulled it out of a cupboard she was tidying. It was in a soft leather pouch with a drawstring, and she opened it up and emptied the necklace out on the table in front of my father and said she didn't know what to do with it.

It was really beautiful. It was creamy white, and each of the beads was carved with a pattern of swirling shapes so it looked like a tightly closed flower bud. Then in the centre there was a single larger bead with three miniature carved elephants on each side of it.

The leading elephants had their foreheads pressed against the big centre bead, as if they were holding it in place. Then behind each of them there was a small elephant, with a very tiny elephant behind that. The following elephants had their trunks twined around the tails of the elephants in front. The carving was so delicate their ears were almost transparent, and they were all perfect. Not one of the sharp little tusks was broken, and I could even see the toenails on their funny round feet.

My mother said it had belonged to my great-grandmother, who had left it to my grandmother, who had given it to her. My father said he was surprised she'd kept it when none of them had liked it or worn it.

I couldn't imagine anyone not liking it.

It was my father who told me it was made of ivory, made from an elephant's tusk. He also told me that my great-grandfather had had it specially made for my great-grandmother. My family has lived in east Africa forever, so I knew it would have been made from an African elephant's tusk, but I didn't think about that, I just thought how much I liked it.

I was going to try it on, but my mother took it away from me and put it back in its bag.

I asked why my great-grandmother didn't like it and my mother said it was because it gave her dreams, but she wouldn't say any more. I think my father would have told me all about it then, but he could see she didn't want him to, so he left it.

I kept thinking about the necklace. I thought about it for days. Then in the end I went and got it out of the cupboard without my parents knowing. I looked at those little elephants again and I thought that if my parents wouldn't tell me about them, perhaps they'd tell me themselves. I decided to sleep with it under my pillow that night, all safe in its leather pouch, and see if it gave me dreams, too.

I was so excited I stayed awake for ages. Then I thought that probably nothing would happen at all and I went to sleep.

When the dream began it was full of a kind of dust storm. All I could see was a golden-yellow, gritty cloud, with little glimpses of twisted thorn trees showing through it. Then, as I watched, I saw that something was moving behind the dust cloud.

At first I wasn't frightened. I felt sure I knew what I would see when the dust cleared, and I was right. A great, grey elephant was walking slowly towards me, past the thorn trees. It was followed by just one very small elephant, which was keeping close to its huge mother.

The dream was totally silent, which was strange. I couldn't hear the wind that had blown the dust cloud away, and I couldn't hear the footsteps of the elephant and her child. Then the big female stopped right in front of me and raised her trunk; and I knew she was trumpeting at me, but I couldn't hear that either.

That's when I began to feel frightened, because I knew the elephant was angry with me – angry and hurt and puzzled, all at the same time.

I wanted to ask her what was wrong, but in the dream I was silent too; I couldn't speak at all. But she was looking at me – staring at me – and I realized I could understand her; I knew what she was telling me.

At that moment there was a loud bang and the elephant shuddered and then swayed and fell, and I woke myself up screaming.

My father ran into my room and said it was all right; it was only a car backfiring. I could hear a car rattling past outside and I heard it give another bang, like a gunshot, as it turned the corner. But even though I believed my father, I said the bang had hurt the elephant. I think I was still partly asleep.

My mother came into the room behind my father and sat on my bed. She told me again that everything was all right and said I must have been dreaming.

I took the pouch out from under my pillow and emptied the necklace onto the duvet; and I said, "The elephant doesn't think it's all right."

My mother said I shouldn't have taken the necklace, but my father said it was time I knew about it. He told me my great-grandfather was a hunter – a poacher, really. He said I mustn't think badly of him, he was just trying to support his family. He shot elephants and sold the tusks to ivory dealers. He kept part of one of the tusks for himself and, when he could afford it, he paid a craftsman to make the necklace.

I said I had to go and see the elephants.

My mother said I'd often seen elephants. But I said that was different; they weren't angry with me then. She said they weren't angry with me now; the necklace had nothing to do with me – it was made years before I was even born.

But the thing was, I knew what the big elephant in my dream had been telling me. She'd wanted me to know that we – my family – had stolen the ivory from her family. I knew I had to find a way to tell her we were sorry.

My father said he'd planned to take us all to the game reserve for the holiday weekend and I'd have to wait till then. Meanwhile he put the necklace back in its bag and back into the cupboard.

I didn't dream the dream again, but I didn't forget it. When it was time to leave for the holiday weekend I went back to the cupboard and took the necklace out of its pouch. It didn't look beautiful to me any more. It wasn't white like cream, it was white like bone, and the little carved elephants seemed like an insult to the wonderful animal who had died so they could be made. I wasn't sure why at the time, but I slipped the necklace into the pocket of my jeans.

The reserve is enormous and in a way it's quite strange. It's a whole piece of Africa set aside for animals, which is great, and most of the time you forget it's also a bit peculiar. Then you see another four-by-four full of tourists and you remember that you're there too, with your camera and binoculars; and none of you belong there. You're just the audience; the people who do belong there have been moved out. All the animals are living their normal lives in their natural habitats – but all the people are either rangers or guides or tourists. Obviously there are no people hunting the animals; but there are no people living in villages or grazing cattle either, which is something they've done for generations. So in one way it's a very natural place, but in another way it's quite unnatural.

Anyhow, that's what I think now, but I don't suppose I thought it then. That first day we saw gazelles, zebra, wildebeest and, in the far distance, a pride of lions resting under a thorn tree. It was the second day before we saw elephants. We were with another group of visitors in a large hide near a water-hole and the elephants came plodding through the undergrowth and waded into the water to drink.

The ranger in charge told us things about them – like that they're the largest land mammals in the world, and that they've been on Earth for thousands of years, and then he pointed out different members of the herd.

I watched, sometimes touching the ivory necklace in my pocket. They drank and wallowed and the younger ones played, pushing each other over and climbing on each other like puppies, and they all used their trunks like hoses to wash their backs.

My mother thought seeing the elephants would make everything all right for me. She said they were having fun, they weren't angry with me. I didn't know how to explain to her that the elephant in my dream wasn't among them, so I didn't say anything.

The ranger drove us back to the lodge, and we picked up our own car and my father began to drive us home again.

Then it happened. Without any warning. We were driving along a rough track, between dense stands of tree and underbrush, and suddenly a great she-elephant pushed through the branches on our left, trunk raised, roaring with rage.

My father braked so suddenly that the car's engine choked and stopped. The elephant was only about two metres away – towering over the car.

And it was her – I knew it was her – the elephant in my dream. I was so frightened I was afraid I was going to be sick.

My mother pointed to the opposite side of the track. There was a small elephant there, watching us rather uncertainly. We were between the mother and her calf.

The big elephant swayed forwards and let out another trumpeting call, full of fury and menace.

My father didn't know what to do. He sat there, clenching his hands on the steering wheel until his knuckles looked as though they'd push right out through the skin. He whispered to us that if he restarted the engine the noise might enrage her even more.

I remember my mother whispering to him, "If she attacks, could she crush the car?" and my father whispering back, "Yes. In seconds."

But I wasn't scared any more because I suddenly knew what I had to do. I pulled the ivory necklace out of the pocket of my jeans, wound down the window, and threw the necklace as far as I could so that it fell in the middle of the track, in front of the car. Then I closed the window quickly.

My father said, "What did you do?" And my mother said, "Start the car – we'll have to risk it now!" But then my father said, "No. Wait. Look!"

The big elephant had turned her head away from us, distracted by what had fallen on the track. At the same time the baby elephant trotted across in front of the car to have a closer look. It pushed the necklace with its trunk – then it picked it up and trotted to its mother's side. She lowered her trunk to stroke it, and then pushed it gently ahead of her into the safety of the underbrush.

At the last moment, she looked back at the car. She didn't seem angry at all. Then both elephants disappeared amongst the trees.

My father started the car in silence, and drove on slowly. Then he told me my trick had worked but that I'd taken a big risk. My mother said she hadn't been able to see whether the young elephant took the necklace or dropped it, but she didn't feel like going back to look. She said she was glad I'd thrown it away with such good effect but it was a shame it was lost.

But it wasn't lost – I'd given it back. It was my great-grandmother's necklace but it was made from *her* grandmother's tusks. I told my parents that, and I know they didn't believe me; and I'm sure you don't believe me either. But I knew, and I still know. I know because she told me in my dream."

CHAPTER SEVEN

Caught up in Hannah's story, no one had noticed Lee's approach. He crouched down in front of them and said softly, and without apparent anger, "You have to learn to be quiet. All of you."

"I'm sorry," said Hannah, feeling her face flaming red. "I thought I was talking quietly."

"The rule," said Lee, "is no talking at all. Any sound may drive away the very creature we hope to see."

"Even if it's underwater?" whispered Hannah.

"Sound is vibration – vibrations move through water," said Lee. "Fishermen do not talk. Since you are clearly not going to rest, you had better come back and watch with me. It is the only position from which to see the whole tarn. But you must be silent."

He stood up and walked back, his feet making no sound. They followed, without a word, treading as carefully as he had.

Staring at the dark, still water was mesmerizing. The moon rose in the sky and seemed to grow smaller but no less bright. Time passed neither slowly nor quickly. They felt as though they were outside time; listening and hearing nothing out of the ordinary; watching and seeing nothing but stillness.

The first movement in the water, the first ripple, could have been caused by a whisper of breeze above or by a small fish below.

Then, a short distance away from that first stirring, something black and shiny broke the surface for a brief moment.

Jake, temporarily in charge of Lee's camera, thought he'd caught it on tape but couldn't be sure. He longed to hand over to Lee, but he knew it was too risky. In the few seconds it would take to change places they could miss a good sighting.

Miguel scrambled to his feet and focused his still camera, hoping the moonlight would be enough.

Jenny dropped down onto her stomach, eyes level with the surface of the tarn, trying to spot the smallest change in the water surface.

Lee cast around with the infrared binoculars, swinging them back and forth across the patch of water where they'd all seen something rise up and sink down again.

Hannah nudged Anya and mimed that Anya should

watch to the right and she would watch to the left.

"There!" whispered Anya.

A narrow path was forming on the surface of the water, dark in the centre and silver at the edges where the moonlight caught the tops of the widening ripples. Something was moving diagonally across the lake, quite fast, towards a large clump of reeds halfway between the promontory and the campsite.

"It's big," Jake mouthed.

"Making for the shore!" whispered Hannah.

"No, for the shallows," said Lee snatching up Jake's camera and running, crouching, to the back of the reed bed for a closer view.

Abruptly, the trail of movement stopped.

"What's the difference between shore and shallows?" said Jenny.

"Water," said Lee, kneeling, waiting, watching.

The next movement was parallel to the reed-lined shore. There was a flurry of water and something broke through. It was black or very dark green, glistening and slimy and muscular, with a small dorsal fin. For a moment it seemed the head would appear, but then the thing turned for the shore again, underwater, and disappear from sight.

And then there was nothing – just more watching, more waiting.

However many times they replayed the footage

Jake and Lee had caught, it told them no more. It was hard to estimate the length of the thing when there was nothing nearby to judge it against, but they all agreed it was about two metres long.

Lee would not be drawn on what he thought it was until he had seen it more clearly. After another hour, he risked talking enough to tell them that though they wouldn't rest before, now they must or they'd be exhausted and no use to him. He said he would stay on watch and wake Jake later to take over for a while. Reluctantly, they walked the short distance back to the camp, this time really intending to try and sleep.

But when Hannah lit the lamp in the tent, they could see that the inside of it looked surprisingly untidy. There was a strange and unpleasant smell hanging around and the cooking equipment, which Hannah had stacked neatly, meaning to store it in the Landrover for the night, had been tipped over.

Then they noticed that the saucepan had disappeared.

Slightly alarmed, they began to check their belongings. Careful searching revealed that two other things were missing – a camera battery pack and a bunch of house keys, belonging to Miguel.

"So what's that all about?" said Anya.

"Whoever it was," said Jenny, wrinkling her nose,

"it was someone who hasn't washed for a long time."

"A vagrant?" said Jake. "But why take the battery pack – it was an old one, dead, used up."

"He might not have known it was dead."

"But it only fits this kind of camera. Are we saying it's a vagrant wildlife film-maker who's burnt a hole in his own pan and doesn't know a dead, dumped battery when he sees it? And why take the keys? There wasn't an address on them, was there?"

"No," said Miguel. "But look."

The zip compartment on the front of his backpack, where the keys had been, had been ripped right across. "Why do that? Why take a knife to it? Why not just undo the zip?"

"Except it wasn't a knife, was it?" said Hannah, kneeling down and peering at the jagged edges of canvas. "Those look like claw marks."

"Oh great," said Anya. "That thing was swimming to the shore. Those two old guys said it sometimes came out of the tarn, remember?"

"I'll tell you something," said Jake, "Even if it gets really warm tomorrow, I'm not bathing in that lake."

"Nor walking in the woods," said Anya.

"Nor sleeping," said Hannah.

"We need to be careful," said Miguel.

"I don't think that needed saying," said Jake.

"No," said Miguel. "I mean we should be careful not

to build on this fear. Fear does strange things to the mind. There's nothing we can do at the moment. None of us wants to track this thing in the dark, and we're never going to guess what it is or why it did what it did. Perhaps in daylight, and with Lee's expertise, we can find out. But now we need to think about something else."

"I think I'd better go and tell Lee," said Jenny, getting to her feet.

"No, wait," said Jake. "He's already had a bit of a go at us, twice. I think we should play it cool. I think it's better to wait till he's done his stint at the lake and comes to get me. Then we can just show him this and tell him what's missing – and see what he thinks."

"We won't have to tell him about the smell," said Anya. "It's gross."

"It's all on this blanket," said Jenny, who'd been investigating on her hands and knees. "Have we got any old food wrappers I can pick it up with? I'll chuck it under the trees."

Hannah went to the Landrover and rearranged the food till she had emptied two plastic carrier bags. Jenny put them on like gloves, scooped up the blanket, ran to the trees and flung it as far away as she could. "Lee can go and smell it over there," she said firmly. "I just hope the vagrant doesn't come back, that's all."

"Vagrants don't have claws," said Anya.

"Things with claws don't steal saucepans and keys," said Jenny. "It must have been a person."

"Animals steal from tents," said Jake. "Trust me, I know. Let's go and sit in the Landrover and I'll tell you about it."

PANDA
Jake's story

"When I was about twelve," said Jake, "I got the chance to go to western China, plant-hunting in an extraordinary area of mountains and forests. I wasn't all that interested in plants, but my dad's a botanist and he was going as assistant to Professor Beall, who was leading the expedition with another scientist called Lao Meng who worked at a research station there. I didn't know till I applied for this trip, but Lao Meng is a good friend of Lee's.

My dad and Professor Beall are both from Brooklyn, but the others were from all over – it was an international expedition and my name was definitely not on the list. But at the last moment the filmy fern expert fell down his porch steps and broke his leg. It was too short notice to get anyone else and my dad suggested taking me, for the experience.

I think the Prof was so surprised he agreed

without thinking, but he began to twitch as soon as the plane was in the air. I remember he said he hoped I wasn't going to run around and trample on rare specimens! As if I was a really little kid. My dad didn't say anything as bad as that but he did say he hoped he wasn't going to regret bringing me. I tried to be really quiet so they'd forget I was there.

The time this thing happened, the Prof, Lao Meng and my dad had left the main expedition to look for a rare species of orchid, and had taken me with them. The plan was for us to go to a remote campsite in the area where they thought the orchids grew. Then Lao Meng would leave us there and collect us in a couple of days.

I remember walking for what seemed like miles through clammy undergrowth in a damp misty forest, among mossy tree trunks, wading through wet ferns and grasses, dodging round thickets of bamboo. It was really tiring.

The Prof kept asking Lao Meng complicated questions about plants, using Latin names. Lao Meng gave complicated answers, but he was really nice to me and kept pointing out things he thought I'd like. I liked the dove tree – the one where the flowers hang down from the branches like handkerchiefs. It was interesting to see bamboo in flower; I don't know if you've seen them, but the blooms are so small and pale they look like pieces of cloth caught on the stems by accident. Lao Meng said the species we saw only flowers once every ten years, so we'd hit the right time.

I was mainly interested in bamboo because I hoped we'd see a panda. The flowering is bad news for them because as soon as the seeds drop the plant dies, and it's years before the new plants are big enough for panda fodder. But there was another species of bamboo in the area which wasn't due to flower for some years, so I thought there just might be pandas around.

One time Lao Meng pointed across a valley and shoved his binoculars at me. I thought he'd seen a panda, but it was a clouded leopard; he called it a mint leopard. It was beautiful. It climbed head first down the trunk of a tree as easily as if it was walking across a meadow. Even though it was so far off, my dad wanted to know if it was dangerous. I think he was wondering how he'd explain to my mom if I got eaten, but Lao Meng said it was only dangerous to monkeys and squirrels and kept well clear of humans. He told me that in ten years of walking in that forest he'd never seen a clouded leopard before. He said I'd brought him luck. He knew the Prof didn't want me there and I'm sure he said that to make me feel better.

The campsite was just a raised wooden platform in a clearing. Lao Meng helped us put up our tents and then headed back and we ate dinner and listened to chirps and shrieks from the forest all around us.

The Prof woke us at dawn. All we could see was mist and ghostly trees. He wanted to leave at once for the orchid search; and he wanted to leave me behind in camp.

I was happy. I was tired of being quiet and careful all the time and I'd got my personal stereo and some good tapes. I hadn't got CDs in those days. Dad was a bit twitchy, but the Prof said I'd be fine and my dad never disagrees with him.

It was great at first, but then time began to go really slowly and by mid-morning I was bored and decided to go for a walk. Ten minutes out from camp I knew I'd made a big mistake.

Shoving through all that dripping undergrowth by myself wasn't at all like following Lao Meng and the others, and though I couldn't see any animals, I had a feeling I was being watched. Then I looked back the way I'd come, and the campsite had disappeared. It was on high ground and I'd thought I'd be able to see it from a long way off; but forests aren't like that.

I crashed back in what I thought was the right direction, hoping the noise would frighten off anything nasty that might be around. I wasn't sure how to explain to a leopard that I wasn't a squirrel or a monkey.

At last I pushed past a stand of bamboo and there

was the tent right in front of me – but there was something, or someone, inside it.

I was sure my dad and the Prof wouldn't be back yet, but I could see movement through the canvas wall, and when I stood still I could hear sounds.

I really wanted to run, but I didn't know where to run to. I crept up to the platform and stood at the foot of the little ladder where I could see into the tent.

Inside, standing with its back to me, was a bear. As I watched, it turned round to face me, sat down, picked up a piece of fruit from the folding table, and ate it. It was black and cream-coloured with little round black ears and smudgy black eyes – yes, folks, it was a panda!

It finished the fruit and saw me, and at once it dropped on all fours. Its mouth was slightly open and I could see strong teeth, like dog's teeth, and long sharp-looking claws on the front feet.

The only pandas I'd seen before were photographs or stuffed toys. This was really different. It was big and I had no idea what it was going to do.

I think I actually talked to it. I said something like, "You shouldn't be in there."

Then I got an idea how to lure it out of the tent. I went back to the bamboo and picked some. The stems were tough and hurt my hands, but I got several and went back to the steps and held them out to the panda.

It sat down again and just went on looking at me.

I inched up the steps, holding out a stem, and when I was close enough the panda reached out a hairy paw, took the stem and started to eat it.

My plan failed totally. I didn't lure the panda out, it lured me in. It just sat where it was, and each time it finished a piece of bamboo it reached out for more. I went back to the thicket several times. I began to feel like a waiter going back and forth from a restaurant kitchen!

When it had eaten enough, it let me scratch it behind the ear with the end of a long stick. Then it let me scratch it with my hand.

I was so overwhelmed that it wasn't either aggressive or afraid that I wanted to give it presents. My hands were bleeding a bit from the bamboo so I offered it some of our fruit and it ate that. Then I gave it some biscuits and finally our store of dried meat. It seemed to like that, which surprised me. I didn't know it then, but they do eat meat sometimes, if they can get it. They don't hunt, but they'll take carrion. We sat side by side. It was big and calm and a bit smelly. Its coat was much thicker and tougher than I'd expected, and it's eyes were really quite small – it's only the dark smudges of fur round them that make them look big.

When it was full it ambled over to my sleeping bag – I was really glad it chose mine. It raked at it with its claws to make a nest, turned round and round, slumped down and went to sleep.

I think I must have watched it for ages before I noticed Professor Beall's spare camera on the table. I could see it was a good one but I was sure the Prof would want a picture, and there was no guarantee the panda would still be there when he and Dad got back.

The click of the shutter woke it, and it got up and ambled across the tent to the opening. I put the camera back on the table and stood out of the way.

Just as it reached the opening, it sat down right beside the table and scratched. The table collapsed and the camera fell.

The panda flopped down the steps and plodded off into the forest. I checked the camera. It was jammed. If only I'd held onto it instead of putting it down.

Even so, I was really impatient for them to get back. When they did, they listened to my story in silence. I thought they were impressed. Wrong!

Professor Beall said, "Cameras can be mended – and most people eat too much when they're bored."

It was a really horrible moment. I said, "You don't believe me – but it's all true."

I looked at my dad. And my dad said, "I was afraid I'd regret bringing you."

Him too!

The Prof said something like, "Forget it. I blame myself for leaving him alone."

And they both began to sort through the specimens they'd brought back.

It got worse. My dad took me aside and told me he was disappointed in me. He said he could forgive me for having a go with the camera and eating so much of the food, but he couldn't forgive me for lying about what had happened.

I tried to show him the claw marks and panda hair on my bedding, but he wouldn't look. He said he wouldn't talk to me again till I admitted the truth.

We ate vegetable stew and rice – it was pretty much all that was left. I took mine away from them and sat on a fallen log. I wasn't at all hungry; I felt sick.

Then I heard something in the forest and I hoped it was Lao Meng come back early. I was sure he'd believe me. But it was better than Lao Meng. It was the panda – back for a refill.

We all stared at it in silence – my dad and the Prof on the platform outside the tent, me on my log on the ground.

The panda plodded towards me. Then it stopped and we looked at each other.

I held out my bowl.

The panda shuffled closer, sniffed the food, then it sat back on its haunches, took the bowl in its paws and drank the stew. Then it licked the bowl thoroughly, inside and out.

No one said a word. No one moved.

When the panda had finished it dropped the bowl, rolled forwards onto all fours and shambled off into the trees.

There was a silence that seemed to last for ages.

Then the Prof said, very quietly, "We have had an honoured guest."

He got up and walked over to me. Then he held out his hand for a formal handshake and said those magic words, "I'm sorry, Jake."

I was pleased but I was really embarrassed. I shook his hand and my dad came up behind him and he apologized too.

And when we got back to New York, someone at the photo lab was able to get the film out of the camera and I'd got a really great shot of the sleeping panda.

But if the panda hadn't come back and the photo hadn't come out, they still wouldn't believe me — and that's a really horrible thought."

CHAPTER EIGHT

Jake's story didn't take long to tell, and when it was over the hours of darkness seemed to stretch ahead forever. Somehow, during the telling, everyone had managed to slump into a more or less comfortable position. Afterwards they didn't talk, they dozed, then woke and shifted cramped limbs, then slept briefly again.

Eventually, guilt crept in.

"We've left Lee out there alone for an awfully long time," said Jenny.

"He did say he'd fetch Jake to take over," said Hannah.

"Yes, but he won't, will he," said Jake. "He doesn't want to hand over to anyone."

"So what do we do?" said Anya.

"We go and offer," said Miguel. "I agree, he won't come back here and sleep, but if we say we'll keep quiet, I think he'll let us stay near him."

He did, and they each found a place to sit on the ground, not too near and not too far.

For a while, they all wished they hadn't bothered.

Keeping watch when nothing is actually happening is always tiring; and staring at the dark, unbroken water was boring. Each time a cloud crossed the face of the moon, dragging a shadow briefly across the tarn in an imitation of water movement, their attention sharpened, and then faded again as they understood what had happened.

The fact that they'd allowed themselves to sleep, however briefly, seemed to make it harder to keep awake now. Each blink became a struggle, the eyelids closing easily enough but not wanting to be lifted open again.

Only Lee seemed tireless. Silently, and without explanation, he moved his camera off the promontory, taking care not to disturb the pair of sleeping ducks. He carried it a short way around the tarn, a little closer to the camp, and set it up again near a small muddy beach, sheltered by rushes. This was more or less the area the tarn creature had seemed to be making for in that brief earlier glimpse.

It looked as though he was expecting it to leave the water after all, despite the fact he had said so firmly it would not. It was not making for the shore, he had said, it was making for the shallows.

Silently, the other five followed him and then

95

settled again, still not too close.

Nothing else happened for a long time, nothing except the occasional rapid flicker of a bat above and the soft sounds from the wood, made by the tiny movements of tree branches, or mice and voles on the needle-covered ground among the roots.

Then first light came, and with it the definite shudder of something moving through the water. Lee said nothing, but somehow they picked up that something had caught his attention and, one by one, they all sat up straighter – then stood, watching.

The same long ripple as before was moving towards them, the water's surface split by well over a metre of something dark and gleaming and sinuous. The movement of the water at each end of the rubbery, slightly mottled back, with its small upright fin, suggested that the whole animal was at least twice as long as the part that showed.

From their position behind and to one side of Lee, they could see that he had his camera trained right on it.

Jake, excitement and urgency making his hands shake and fumble, took up his own camera and fixed the near end of the swimmer in the centre of his lens.

But even though they were all watching, all waiting, all expecting, it was still a shock when the head appeared.

First the body of the tarn monster sank out of sight. Next they all noticed the frogs. Some were on land near the edge of the water, probably just back from a night of hunting among the rough grass and scattered plants, and probably responsible for some of the soft night noises. Some were in the water, among the reeds, resting, the tops of their heads and their eyes visible above the surface.

They were so distracted by the frogs that when the head did appear, they were taken totally by surprise.

The head was hideous, broad and flat, a murky, greenish-black colour, fish-like but with no scales. The eyes were tiny but the mouth was large and wide-open. It snatched up several frogs and instantly submerged. The water shuddered and the thing was gone.

"What was *that*?" said Jenny.

Lee straightened up and stretched his back. He turned to Jake calmly and asked, "Did you get it?"

"I think so. Like Jenny says, what is that thing?"

Lee replayed his footage. With the shock value gone, they were able to look at it in more detail. They had seen the flat, evil-looking head and the wide mouth easily enough before, now they noticed it had something almost like a beard of four short protrusions growing out of its chin, and two long ones growing from each side of its great mouth.

"Some weird fish," said Jake.

"And big," said Jenny. "Very big. A monster."

"It is said they can grow to five metres," said Lee, "but I estimate this one is two metres long, or maybe a little more."

"Is it what you thought it was?" said Hannah.

"It is what I suspected. Do none of you have any ideas? The four barbels on its lower jaw and the two on the upper – a little like whiskers, yes?"

"A catfish?" said Anya.

"A European catfish, sometimes called a Wels catfish," said Lee. "Imported at some time, probably when young and small. It is at least sixty years old now, I would think."

"But if it's been here for sixty years…" began Jenny.

"Unlikely," said Lee. "It would have been talked about sooner. It has probably been in the ornamental lake of some grand house or castle, but when it began to eat too many ornamental ducks a decision was made to find it a new home. A guess, but I think a good one."

"So someone just brought it out and dumped it here?" said Anya, sounding shocked.

"It happens."

"But when it runs out of ducklings and coots and frogs…?"

"It won't. It has eaten well and will probably rest for a long time now. It can sleep in the mud for weeks without stirring and in the winter it will hibernate for months. The birds will probably raise a new brood this year. They are used to losing chicks, one way or another, and trying again. And the next brood, and most of the adults, are likely to survive the tarn monster."

"So we've got it," said Jake, his voice flat and low.

"We have it on tape," said Lee. "A hat trick is the expression, I believe! We have the parakeets, the mink and now a Wels catfish. When we get back to London, we have one day in an editing suite and we will edit this into something so exciting, I shall have a good chance of getting the funding to make a real film."

They looked at him in silence.

"What is the matter?" said Lee. "You don't like to succeed?"

"I can't explain it," said Jake. "Maybe it's just tiredness – but I feel kind of disappointed."

Anya nodded. "It's not a mystery any more," she said. "Just a big ugly fish."

"Ah," said Lee. "You prefer the journey to the destination. Well, our next journey is back to London and then we all go our own ways. That is the best I can offer you, I'm afraid. We had allowed another day here but now we don't need it; we could go at once, but no one is fit to drive – we all need sleep. So, back to camp to sleep – and then we go."

"Oh," said Jenny. "There's something about the camp you don't know yet."

Lee inspected the ripped pocket on Miguel's backpack, allowed himself to be led to the abandoned blanket to sniff its unpleasant, musty smell, and listened as they told him about the saucepan, the used battery pack and the house keys that were missing.

Apart from asking if they were quite sure they hadn't mislaid the missing objects, he said nothing, but looked thoughtful.

"We were never far from the tent," said Anya. "Even over on the promontory we were still really close. It must have been very quiet."

"Maybe it was the ghost of the Monk of Monk's Tarn," said Jake cheerfully.

"It has to have been a person," said Jenny. "I don't mean a ghost, obviously; I mean a tramp, a vagrant. Probably going to make a fire in the wood and wanting a pan to cook in. Maybe he was going to take the blanket but realized we were close and dropped it."

"What about the smell?" said Anya.

"If he wrapped it round himself before he dropped it – vagrants aren't exactly known for being clean – that could account for it."

Lee said nothing.

"But, Jenny," Miguel objected, pointing to the ripped backpack, "a person would have undone that, or possibly cut it with a knife, not clawed it open!"

"I've been thinking about that," said Jenny. "I think

you probably got it caught on a tree branch and it tore and the keys fell out."

"I haven't walked through the woods with the pack," said Miguel. "We drove here."

"Yes, I mean before this trip. Last time you used the backpack. And you just didn't notice. That could happen."

"I would have noticed that I'd lost my keys."

"But would you? Think – do you share with anyone?"

"Yes. There are four of us in a student apartment."

"Well, if each time you got home – after you lost them – there was always someone in, you wouldn't need your keys and you might not realize they'd gone."

Miguel shook his head. "I'd have noticed that rip when I packed to come here," he said, but Jenny ignored him.

One by one the group disappeared discreetly into the woods and then returned and collected tarn water for a cursory wash.

Hannah was last. She wanted to set up everything first, ready to put together some kind of breakfast, because Lee had said it would be a good idea to eat before they slept.

When everything was ready, she walked along the path by the trees before ducking into the wood, just as the others had, to choose a place at a discreet distance from the camp.

The light was still pale and misty, but beginning to strengthen now. The ducks and coots and moorhens were diving and feeding, apparently unaware of the predator underneath.

She turned into the woods, treading on the soft carpeting of pine needles, and found a neat and private little clearing.

Later, as she left the clearing, she saw that she had walked further in among the trees than she had realized. Not much light ever penetrated the forest floor, but with the sun so low it seemed particularly gloomy. Still, through gaps between the trunks there were glimpses of grey, glittering water to show her the right direction.

And then she saw it. It was between her and the path, which was about four metres away.

It was impossible to tell its size – it blended with the shadows. It stood four-square, facing her. Then it bared its teeth and growled.

CHAPTER NINE

By the time Hannah got back to the camp she had slowed her run to a walk. "I've seen it!" she said. "The thing in the wood. It's back there."

She couldn't remember how she'd got past it, but she had done it somehow, running silently on soft needles, not breathing till she was out from under the trees and could see that it was not following her.

"But we know it doesn't come out of the lake," said Jenny, frowning. 'Whatever those old guys said about it, it doesn't. It can't. You've seen it. It's a fish."

"It's not the catfish," said Hannah. "It's something else. Come on, quickly."

They all followed her, trying to be quick and quiet at the same time. Nevertheless, and even though Hannah was certain she'd found the right place, there was nothing to be seen there.

They were going to spread out to search, but Lee,

stooping low to examine the place Hannah had indicated, called them back. He said that if the animal Hannah had seen had left tracks or traces, five pairs of feet would obliterate them.

"Describe it," he said to Hannah as they all walked back to the camp.

"It was as big as a large dog," said Hannah, "but a different shape. It was on all fours and it snarled at me. I could see its teeth."

"What colour?"

"I don't know. It's quite dark under the trees. Black or brown. With light marks on its face."

"A badger," said Jenny. "There must be badgers here after all."

"You said there weren't," said Jake.

"I was told there weren't," said Jenny. "But..." She make a rueful little face, "there must be more than one dog attacking sheep, and I didn't hear about that either."

"It wasn't a badger," said Hannah impatiently. "It was bigger than a badger and – I don't know – different, quite different. *Not* a badger."

Jenny sat down on the ground sheet, beside the stove and the kettle of water Hannah had set out, and reached out a hand to pull Hannah down beside her. "The thing is," she said, "we're all really tired and we all feel a bit lost now we've caught the tarn monster on tape, and woods are always full of shadows."

"Don't you believe me?" said Hannah, resisting the pull of Jenny's hand and remaining standing.

"Woods are full of shadows," Jenny repeated, in an infuriatingly reassuring voice, "and full of sounds. And being very tired is as bad as being drunk; perception gets all messed up."

"You *don't* believe me!" said Hannah.

"I believe you," said Jake.

"I'm sure you do," said Jenny.

"What's that supposed to mean?"

"Well, you've had experience of not being believed and you know what it's like."

"And I was right!"

"Yes, but come on. It can't have been a dog or a fox, Hannah would have recognized it; so what other option is there, in England? A badger. And OK, it looked a bit different in the shadows under the trees – but mistakes are easy to make and, Hannah, you are an imaginative person. We know that from your story of the dreams about elephants."

Lee watched them silently.

Jake said, "Just because she has imagination, doesn't mean she can't see reality."

"Of course not," said Jenny. "But people built rumours and scare stories around the Wels catfish, and we now know they were just stories. It's huge and greedy, but it doesn't climb out on land and savage sheep."

"OK," said Jake. "It wasn't the tarn monster. Hannah said that — she knows it wasn't the fish. But perhaps it was the thing that came into camp and took stuff away and clawed great gashes in Miguel's backpack."

"That was a tramp," said Jenny.

"You know that, do you? And what about the thing that is attacking sheep? Something is. No one's going to imagine a dead sheep with its throat torn out."

"Just because they shot one dog," said Jenny, "doesn't mean that there can't be another. Listen, I'm not being nasty to Hannah, it's easy to make a mistake in a shadowy wood. And she can't even describe it, can she?"

"Have you both finished talking about me as if I'm not here?" said Hannah. "Because if so I'd just like to say that I *have* been in England for a month now, and I *have* been badger watching; I know what badgers look like and I would have recognized one in the darkest part of the wood. No, I can't describe it properly, but I know what it wasn't, and it was *not* a badger. Or a dog, either."

"Hannah," said Miguel, "tell me about it and I'll try to draw it. You can correct me as I go."

"Great," said Jake, his face relaxing into a smile. "An identikit picture."

Miguel fetched his sketchpad and he and Hannah sat on the groundsheet facing each other, with Jake and Anya beside them. Jenny busied herself making tea. Lee stood behind Miguel, watching over his shoulder as he drew.

"I will make a rough sketch, while you talk," said Miguel, "then I will show you and we will correct it. So – shaped like a dog, you say?"

"Not exactly. It was on all fours, but wider across the back than most dogs. And it was sort of crouching, so its front legs looked longer than the back, though they probably weren't. But it was crouching like a cat does when it's going to spring."

"The head?"

"Oh," said Hannah, "this is the hard bit. I don't know – I know it had teeth, its mouth was open and I could see them. It growled at me."

"You surprised it," said Jake. "You scared it. Probably just defensive growling."

"No," said Hannah firmly. "It wasn't scared. *I* was. It was threatening me."

"The head?" said Miguel. "The eyes?"

"Small eyes, I think. I didn't really see the eyes properly, but it had a pale colour across its head."

"Above the eyes?"

"I think so. Can't be sure."

"And the shape of the head?"

"Round. With small ears. But no, it had a muzzle like a dog – and the teeth were like dogs' teeth. And claws, it had claws – big feet, kind of splayed out so the claws showed. Maybe it didn't have small ears, maybe the ears were flattened against its head like a cat's ears when it's angry. In a way it was a bit like a bear – not nearly so big; but big enough."

"So it was a mixture of a cat and a dog and a bear," said Jenny as she poured hot water onto tea bags.

"Don't send her up," said Jake.

Then Miguel leant forward and passed his rough sketch to Hannah. "Tell me from this," he said. "Tell me what to alter."

Hannah took it and looked down at the picture. He had sketched a four-legged shape, crouching menacingly, with long claws protruding from its feet – and with two heads.

Hannah shoved it back at him, her face like thunder. "Now *you're* sending me up," she said.

"Don't get hysterical," said Jenny, handing her a mug of tea which she ignored.

"No," said Miguel, taking the sketch from her but holding it out so she could still see it. "No, Hannah, I'm not, I promise."

"She never said it had two heads," said Jake angrily. "You're not being fair."

"And I never said it had claws a foot long like that," said Hannah. "Just ordinary long, sharp claws – claws that were showing, not retracted."

"I will make the claws shorter," said Miguel patiently. "And the heads are alternatives for you to choose from. Look, one that is rounder and flatter and the other with a longer muzzle. One with small, round ears and the other with larger ears that are flattened on the head. One with the pale line above the eyes, the other with the pale line across the eyes, like a mask."

"Oh," said Hannah. "I see. Sorry."

"Yeah, sorry, Miguel," said Jake.

"The trouble is," said Hannah, "I can't choose. I didn't stay looking at it. Neither of those heads is right, but I can't tell you what's wrong with them. I really am sorry, Miguel, I know you're trying to help."

"It's OK," said Miguel, with a shrug.

Lee, accepting a mug of tea from Jenny, said, "There is one thing none of you has checked."

They looked at him.

"The scent," said Lee. "I smelt the ground where Hannah says the animal was standing. I caught the same animal-scent that was on the blanket. It was faint, but it was there."

"So you believe me?" said Hannah.

"I will go and search for signs," said Lee, not answering her directly. "I have a better chance if I go alone. It is possible I can track it from the point where Hannah left it. In the meantime, I think everyone should settle down. It is not good if arguments begin within a team. As soon as I find anything – any indication of what might be living in the wood – I will come back and tell you. I will not let you miss anything."

"Be careful," said Hannah.

"I am always careful," said Lee.

"That man never seems to need rest or food," said Jenny, as he walked off.

"I guess it comes with practice," said Jake doubtfully. "And you may have to admit you're wrong, Jenny, because Lee is interested and Lee isn't the kind of man to look for the tracks of an imaginary beast."

Jenny sighed. "OK," she said, surprising them all. "I could be wrong. It happens." She smiled. "Not often, but it happens. It just didn't sound very believable."

"If you want to hear something that's really unbelievable," said Anya, "I could tell you how I got interested in wildlife, and especially in working with sound."

"Go on," said Hannah.

"It's not at all convincing," said Anya, "but it is true."

WHALE
Anya's story

"My parents come from Hawaii," said Anya, "but I wasn't born there. I was born in Detroit, where my parents were working. We moved back to Hawaii when I was eleven, so although it was where I belonged, it was all new to me.

We got a boat, a little cabin cruiser, so we could go across from the big island, where we lived, to the island where my grandmother had her house. We'd been before, in daylight both ways, but this time, a sudden storm blew up while we were with Grandma. By the time it was safe to leave, it was dark, and though the storm was over, the lightning was still flickering in the distance, just where the sky meets the sea.

The sea looked much deeper at night than it did in the daytime, and it also looked wider and stronger – and stranger. It wasn't rough, there weren't any waves beating against the boat; but the sea was making big slow movements under us, as if it was breathing long slow breaths, or as if something enormous was moving just under the surface. The lights of our home harbour looked as tiny and distant as stars.

The storm clouds had cleared and the moon was enormous and really bright. My mother said it was a magic night now the storm was over. I thought it was scary and I asked her if she meant good magic or bad magic, but I don't think she answered me.

She was driving the boat and my father was trying to make the radio work properly. The storm had left the air full of electricity and the words were coming out of it all mixed up with sparkling noises. It sounded as though a thousand needles were being shaken in a glass box. We couldn't hear the news report very clearly, but we could hear enough to know that an oil tanker had run aground in the bad weather. The crew had been rescued but a huge oil slick was already spreading.

We all knew what that meant – fish choked to death and seabirds with oil on their wings and beaks so they wouldn't be able to fly or feed. It could even catch light and send a firestorm across the surface of the sea. I was scared we were going to get caught in it, but my parents said it was a long way away.

I watched the water and I remember that it was then that I really understood why people used to believe in sea monsters. It really did look as though something huge was moving just below the surface, making the sea bulge up and down. My father said it was the effect of the current and my mother said it was the pull of the moon. But suddenly I saw something that really frightened me; something enormous had risen up out of the water behind us and then sunk down again. Something much, much bigger than the tarn monster.

My parents hadn't seen it and when they looked where I pointed, I couldn't see it either. But I was sure it was coming closer – underneath.

My mother said not to panic, and she slowed the boat and let it drift a little sideways so she could look behind us.

We all saw it at the same time – a dark mass that rose up through the surface of the water in the moonlight and then sank again.

My parents knew at once that it was a whale, even before they got out the binoculars. If I'd lived there a bit longer I would have, too. My father told me it was a humpback whale, but he said it didn't look right. It was floating and sinking instead of swimming and diving.

My mother said she was sure it was in trouble. She thought it might be injured in some way.

Then it was my turn with the binoculars, and I saw there was something else there as well as the humpback whale – something smaller. And then I knew, it was her baby.

My mother said she could guess what had happened, and I can remember exactly how her voice sounded – as if she really wished she couldn't. She said the tanker must have broken up in the breeding grounds. The whale had recently had her calf and then she'd had to out swim the oil slick and she was exhausted.

I asked if she'd be all right, and at first neither of them answered me. We watched as she and the baby surfaced and slowly sank again, and then my father said things looked bad. He said he didn't think she had enough strength left to keep herself and her calf at the surface. He said, "Whales breathe air, like us. I think she may be drowning." Then he turned back to the radio.

I was horrified. I said we had to do something. But my mother put her arms round me and told me there was nothing we *could* do. The whale was enormous and very heavy – there was no way we, in our little boat, could possibly support her while she rested. My mother said we must go home and she began to rev the engine up again.

I said we couldn't just go away and leave her, knowing she was in trouble, but my mother said, "We can't help; and I don't want to watch them both die."

My father said he was trying to get the coastguard on the radio, in case anyone else could do anything, but he couldn't get through.

I saw the whale's back again, but she didn't rise as

116

far out of the water as she had before and she was gone again almost at once. I didn't see her calf at all.

My mother was looking back as well and she said, "She's not blowing, she's not breathing. We have to go."

It was so terrible. I felt so desperate. I wanted to scream; and I did scream – I screamed and shouted at the moon, "Save her, do something, please!"

The moon shone on the water – and then there were strange sounds, coming from everywhere and nowhere. There were trumpeting sounds – almost like elephants, but not elephants – and strong, steady chirping sounds like birds – but not birds.

My mother said, "What's that?" and cut the engine.

The sounds grew stronger. They shivered through the sky, as though the moonlight had a voice. They echoed deep under the water and made the boat shudder.

And then we saw! Far behind, and way over to each side of us, the water seemed to be alive. Great shapes were breaking the surface, gleaming silver in the moonlight. Waterspouts were glittering up into the air. Massive tails were flicking upwards and then sinking in slow, deep dives.

Whales were coming.

My father said it must be the rest of the herd.

They were enormous and powerful and they surged through the water at astonishing speed – yet somehow everything seemed dreamlike.

My father said we should get into shore because they could sink us; but he didn't move. And my mother agreed with him, but she didn't move either.

And as we watched, the nearest whales submerged and then rose up again, very slowly, very steadily, lifting the mother and her calf between them.

My mother said she'd heard of something like this, of whales rescuing each other, though I could hardly hear her words because the whale songs were so loud.

The four whales that were acting as supporters lay still and steady on the surface. The rest swam and dived almost as though they were playing – the weird thing was that in spite of their massive size, they didn't make any waves; our little boat didn't rock.

Then my father said, "More are coming, but they're not all the same kind." And they weren't. We saw humpback whales, with long flippers and tiny back fins; the smooth backs of great right whales; the huge, blunt head of a sperm whale; and, in the distance, a basking blue whale, so vast that it looked like a small island. There was even a narwhal, with a single corkscrew tusk, like a sea unicorn.

My mother said, "I don't understand what's happening."

Something else was odd too. As the whales moved in the water, we could see great, dark gashes in their sides. Some of them even had harpoons buried deep in their bodies with the shafts sticking out at odd angles.

Every one of the whales around the female and her calf was badly injured, but not one of them seemed to mind.

My mother said it was the strangest sight anyone ever saw, and I thought she was right. I thought it was magic.

Afterwards none of us could remember how many whales we saw that night and none of us could remember how long the female humpback took to recover. But we were all sure of one thing; the second she began to move on – the second she didn't need help any more – every one of the other whales vanished. I mean really vanished. They didn't swim away or submerge; they just weren't there any more.

When we got back we heard a report on local radio that a female humpback and a calf had been sighted, swimming towards the south, well away from the oil slick. My parents asked around, but no one had seen what happened; we were the only ones who had seen the spirits of the dead whales coming to help her.

And I said it wasn't scientific – and I know you won't believe me – but that's what happened. But imagine if I could have recorded all those whale songs, all different, all in the same place at the same time…"

CHAPTER TEN

As Anya finished, Lee stepped from between the pines into the brightening daylight. His expression was as calm as usual, but he stopped just short of the camp and beckoned to them.

"You've found something?" said Hannah, scrambling to her feet.

Lee didn't answer her, but walked back in among the trees. They followed, silently and in single file.

The carpeting of pine needles was not a good surface for tracking, but Lee pointed at the ground a couple of times. They looked where he indicated, they looked at each other, they shook their heads. Whatever he had noticed was hidden from them.

Then he stopped in a tiny clearing, created where a pine had died and crashed down taking two others with it. Brambles were creeping over the fallen trunks and something was caught on a cluster of thorns. As they looked more carefully, they saw similar pale tufts caught on thorns a little further away.

Jenny bent down, pulled the nearest one free and held it out on the palm of her hand. "Sheep wool," she said.

"*Sheep* wool?" said Jake. "So are we looking for a were-sheep here?"

Lee was still glancing from the brambles to the five of them, clearly waiting for someone to notice something else.

Hannah leant across the nearest trunk and reached out to point. The morning sun was still very low and the light in the clearing was not good. Even so, it was just possible to see something else caught on the brambles – a few coarse, dark hairs, a little like dog hairs.

Hannah screwed up her nose. "When you bend down near the ground," she said, "you can smell it. Same as the rug, but not nearly so strong."

They looked at Lee, but he just indicated that they should follow him again, on through the woods to another tiny clearing. Here, the latrine shovel was leaning where he had left it against a nearby tree. There was a newly dug shallow hole in the ground – and a stink that caught at the backs of their throats.

"This burial is recent," said Lee. "It was easy to see the disturbed earth and easy to move it aside." He seemed unperturbed by the smell.

They moved closer and looked into the shallow trench. There lay the missing saucepan, the used battery pack, Miguel's keys, and a large chunk of raw meat with earth clinging to it and sharp broken ribs sticking out. Lee kicked it over onto its other side. It looked slightly less macabre when the side covered in matted sheep wool was uppermost.

"At least we know it's not part of a person," said Anya.

"It has been butchered," said Lee, "but not with skill or finesse. Nevertheless, it is easy to see it is half a lamb, a few weeks old I would think."

"So it was left here by a vagrant?" said Jenny cautiously.

Miguel picked his keys up gingerly, smelt them, looked around in vain for something to wipe them on, and then hooked the key ring over one finger and held them away from him.

"No," said Lee. "All this was buried – stored – by an animal. In fact almost certainly by the animal Hannah heard, and later saw. Anyone have any ideas?"

"You know, don't you?" said Hannah.

"I have a strong suspicion."

"Care to share it?" said Jake.

Lee smiled. "I have already tracked on your behalf," he said. "I don't intend to think for you as well." His eyes were very bright. "We will not leave today," he said. "This animal is nocturnal, so tonight we try to capture it on tape. If it is what I think it is, it is not a native of the British Isles. I do not know how it came to be here, but it is an Alien Invader; and if it is in our pilot, it will be the star."

They stood quietly, looking down at the strange burial.

It was very silent in the wood; the trees blocked all the sounds from outside, even the persistent calling of the coots. In that brief moment of stillness, when they stood without speaking, looking at the strange burial in front of them, they all heard the same thing. It was a quiet, regular sound, drawing closer – the soft padding feet of an approaching animal.

Lee frowned, and Jake looked wildly round, noting that the only one with a camera was Miguel; and that was only a still camera.

The footsteps paused, then advanced. A moment later, a sheepdog pushed through into the clearing. At once it stopped, flattened its ears, then turned and fled.

"Someone around," said Lee briskly, striding off after it. "We should not have left the camp unattended. My fault."

"That dog was really frightened of us," said Hannah, hurrying in his wake. "I think it must have been ill-treated."

"It was frightened," said Lee, "but probably not of us."

A tall man in jeans and a sweatshirt was waiting for them at the camp. The sheep dog stood by him, ears up, looking anything but cowed. A second sheep dog was nearby. The man was carrying a shotgun over one arm, the barrel pointing safely to the ground.

He nodded to them in quite a friendly way and said, "A lamb was taken last night from one of my fields behind the wood. Just wanted to ask – have you seen a stray dog anywhere around?"

"No," said Lee truthfully.

Miguel went to the edge of the tarn to wash his keys. The farmer didn't notice.

"Are you carrying mobiles?" he asked.

"We are," said Lee.

The farmer pulled some scraps of paper out of the breast pocket of the sweatshirt and handed one to him. "This is my number," he said. "If I'm out my wife'll be home, or there's an answer machine. Will you let me know if you do see anything?"

"We will report any stray dogs," said Lee, putting the piece of paper into his pocket.

"Or anything else," said the farmer. "Any kind of lair where it might be hiding up." He nodded towards the equipment in the Landrover. "Looks as if you're filming," he said. "If you're looking for locations in the woods, you want to be careful. If it's the same dog as killed one of my ewes a week ago, it's got powerful jaws and it's strong. It almost bit the head off and it dragged the carcass right to the edge of the wood. I could see the blood trail in the grass. Took it about thirty metres, and she was a heavy old girl."

"Didn't your dogs do anything?" said Hannah.

"It was just before first light," said the farmer. "The dogs were still in the outhouse. But they must have heard something because they set up a right commotion. I got my gun and let 'em out and I could see the flock was all over our side of the field, close up together. The dogs were late in their warning though. They led me to the old ewe and then lit off into the woods – but it was too late for her. Anyhow, the dogs had the scent of something. I followed 'em. I thought they'd corner it and I could finish it off. But I met 'em coming back, tails between their legs, looking as if they'd been whipped. I reckon they did corner it, but whatever it was, they didn't want to tangle with it. They're working dogs, not guard dogs, but they're good old boys. They're not cowards. It's got to be one big dog."

"You're sure it's a dog?" said Lee.

"What else could it be? A fox might take a newborn, but it wouldn't take a full-grown ewe. And foxes are cowards. There's no way one would see off my dogs. Anyhow, it won't happen again. It's ranged all over this area and I'm taking action. I've hired a couple of heavies, arriving today. If it comes to my field again it'll be seen off."

"Will they have shotguns?" said Anya, nervously, wondering how close to their camp the heavies might range.

The farmer laughed. "No," he said. "Unarmed heavies."

They watched as the farmer headed off to circle the wood, his good old boys at his heels.

When he judged him to be out of earshot, Lee said, "That dog wasn't afraid of us back there. It caught the scent of the animal that buried the lamb and it didn't want to face it a second time."

"I'm not sure I want to face it a first time," said Jenny.

"Hannah faced it and survived," said Jake. "It's powerful, this imaginary animal of Hannah's, isn't it, Jenny? Kills sheep and lambs, rips open backpacks, scares off dogs…"

"All right," said Jenny. "I was wrong. I'm really sorry, Hannah. It just didn't seem very likely; but I should have believed you."

"It's OK," said Hannah. "I didn't really believe me myself."

"Now," said Lee, "we sleep and then we eat. And then we hunt."

Not one of them expected to sleep, but having lost pretty well a whole night, exhaustion ensured that they did. Lee woke them a couple of hours before dusk and suggested a full equipment check and then a meal, which would still give them time to get into position before the light died away.

"Did you sleep at all?" asked Jake suspiciously.

"No," said Lee. "I have been walking. Around and through the wood." He smiled. "And the farmer's heavies are indeed in place. Now – we need bait."

"We bought two small cooked chickens," said Hannah. "It could have one of those and we can share the other. I'll make extra bean and vegetable gloop to go with it."

"But will it want anything?" said Anya. "It ate half a lamb last night and it has the rest in its larder."

"Plus a pan to cook it in," said Jake. "What kind of animal takes a pan – and keys?"

"One that likes to collect things," said Lee. "And it is greedy. It is a glutton. I think it is unlikely to miss the chance of an extra free meal."

When all the equipment had been checked and all batteries renewed, Jenny, Jake and Anya sat with Hannah, watching as the gloop reached simmering point. Miguel sat near them, sketching. Lee stood apart, looking at the sky, checking the height of the sun against his watch.

"He's always off by himself," muttered Jake, looking across to where Lee stood, quite separate, apparently unaware of them.

"He's used to working alone," Hannah whispered back. "He probably finds it a real trial having five of us following him everywhere."

"So how come he advertised for us?"

"He got educational funding," said Jenny softly. "We came with the money. And it has been a great opportunity, hasn't it?"

"Fair enough," said Jake.

"Food won't be long," called Hannah, raising her voice to reach Lee.

He nodded. "Good," he said. He didn't move.

Miguel held his sketchpad out towards them. "Which head?" he said. "It's from memory and I'm not sure I've remembered it accurately."

He had drawn the Wels catfish, at the moment that its head and most of its back were out of the water, its mouth gaping to snatch a frog. Between them, they talked him through adjusting the sketch until everyone was satisfied with it.

"Miguel, I'm sorry I had a go at you earlier," said Hannah, "when you drew two heads for the thing in the wood. I just didn't understand how you work. I do now – I can see it's a good way."

"No problem," said Miguel. "I need to get things right if I can, especially if they're frightening. Making a likeness of a thing pins it down and gives you a kind of control over it."

"Control?" said Jenny, raising her eyebrows.

Miguel smiled. "I don't really mean control over the animal itself, I mean control over your fear of it. That's how I discovered I could draw."

"How do you mean?" said Hannah.

"My teacher at school – Mr Santos – it was when he taught me how to deal with fear. Then he was the one who encouraged me to go to art school in the US. He's the reason I'm here, really, because I then got the chance to do an exchange trip with a UK student, saw Lee's ad and asked if I could join in."

"Hey," said Jake, "you're the only one who hasn't told us how you got into this wildlife thing. Now's a good time – while we eat dinner."

EAGLE
Miguel's story

"I think I was younger than the rest of you when it happened," said Miguel. "I was soon to be ten years old. Our teacher, Mr Santos, took four of us for a two-day trek into the forest. I was the youngest of the group. I knew it was a great privilege. We four were chosen because we had got good marks in the end of term exams.

We were not going to put up tents. At night we were to stay safely at a logging encampment. Even so, to the four of us who were used to living in the city, it was a real adventure and everyone was very excited.

We had to walk a long way, or it seemed long to us. Often we followed the wide tracks left by the logging companies, but still the forest was all around us.

There was an eagle, a Philippines eagle, gliding above the forest canopy. His shadow moved across the trees underneath him, and when he was above the wide track where we were, his shadow moved across us as well.

When the shadow passed over me I felt as though the bird himself had touched me, had seen me with his sharp eagle's eyes. I ducked down, even though he was so high, and then I looked round quickly to see if the others had noticed; but they hadn't, they were all standing still, looking up.

Mr Santos asked if we had ever seen such a sight before, and we said we had not. "Very magnificent," he said. "And now very rare, sadly."

We walked on and I knew that of all of us, I was the only one who was not happy. The forest was full of strange clickings, rustlings and sudden screeches of unseen forest animals. The towering trees and the confusion of tangled undergrowth made me feel small and scared. I wanted to be as brave and happy as the others, but the forest seemed to me to be full of menace. And then, as the shadow of that massive bird of prey passed over me a second time and then a third, it began to seem to me like the spirit of the forest itself – warning me, threatening me.

Mr Santos pointed out all kinds of things – we even found a reticulated python hanging in loops on a branch and everyone admired the rich patterns on its skin from a safe distance. But I hardly looked; I was watching the patches of sky above, hoping the eagle would not return a fourth time.

The sky remained empty and I followed as Mr Santos led us to a twisted tree that grew half wrapped around its neighbour. The figs on its branches were just beginning to ripen. Mr Santos said we should stay out of sight, keep quiet and watch what came to feed. So in spite of the ants and insects, we did; we waited until we felt quite dizzy with the steamy, green smell of the jungle.

A hornbill came first, tearing at the tree with its great beak and then throwing back its head to roll the fruit down its throat. Then there were more of them. And then we heard a chittering sound, and Mr Santos whispered that it meant macaque monkeys were near.

I looked up, hoping to see them.

And it was there! The eagle! High on a branch at the edge of the clearing, quite still, its shape clearly outlined against the sky.

I gave a shout that sent the hornbills clattering away into the distance.

Mr Santos didn't tell me off, he just asked what was the matter. I pointed to the eagle and tried to explain that I knew it was watching me.

Mr Santos said it was true it was watching. But it wasn't watching me, it was hunting for lemurs or flying squirrels.

I said I wished it would hunt somewhere else, in some other part of the forest. And so Mr Santos explained about the logging. He said so many trees had been felled and taken that the patch of forest we were in had become like an island. He said the eagle was a forest bird and couldn't hunt anywhere else.

The eagle spread his wings and flapped slowly out of sight.

"There, it's gone!" said Mr Santos.

I tried to speak so the others couldn't hear. I tried to convince Mr Santos that it would come back. I told him I knew it was out to get me.

He was kind, but he told me I was afraid of the jungle because it was unknown territory. He was looking out for us, he said, and there was no danger to us from the eagle. I think that was when he told me about the two kinds of fear. He said there is fear of danger, which is useful because it makes you protect yourself; and there is fear of fear itself, which is not useful. And he told me that I was suffering fear of fear; and that if I didn't do something about it that kind of thing could ruin my life. He said I should let go of my fear.

He had been speaking softly, and the hornbills were beginning to return to the figs. He pointed to them – they are extraordinary birds, you know – and he said I shouldn't spoil all this for myself.

I agreed with him and said I was all right now. But I wasn't.

The leader of the macaque monkeys appeared, clinging to a rope of liana, drawn by the scent of the ripe figs but wary of us. The rest of the troop was high out of sight, but we could hear it rustling and chattering overhead.

Suddenly something went crashing through the top branches like a powerful wind. It made all of us jump; the macaques shrieked and their leader ran howling up the liana-rope and vanished among the branches. We could hear a violent chase – invisible, hidden by all the foliage. Then it stopped, and in the silence a few torn leaves drifted down.

Mr Santos asked if we knew what had happened.

We did. We had guessed. One of the others said it was the eagle, and someone asked if it got a monkey. Someone else said it sounded like a monster.

I remember I said nothing at all. I was shaking.

Mr Santos patted me on the shoulder and said, "The monkey may have escaped, but we have to be realistic. The eagle needs to eat and it probably has young to feed."

I just shook my head. I couldn't speak. I felt total horror – and it wasn't only because of the monkey.

The other boys were a bit older than me and they were nice to me; they didn't tease me. They told Mr Santos I thought the eagle was haunting me and one of them said it had bewitched me.

Mr Santos said I had bewitched myself. And then – I will never forget this – he told me he would teach me how to break the spell. He picked up a long stick and scuffed a clear patch on the dusty ground with his foot. Then he handed me the stick and told me to draw the eagle.

Everyone was watching me. I took the stick and just stared at the patch of earth – and then I knew how to do it. I drew it the way I'd first seen it, the way its shadow had fallen on me. I drew an enormous outline, with the powerful wings at full stretch and the head to one side so the great beak showed.

"Good," said Mr Santos. And it was good; it was a good picture.

Then he told me to look carefully at the picture. He said that what I had drawn was not the eagle itself but my fear of the eagle. And he told me to cross it out.

I hadn't known I could draw like that, and a little part of me didn't want to spoil it. But at the same time I hated it and didn't want it to stay there. So I took the stick in both hands, stabbed one end of it into the earth near the head, and crossed the whole thing out in one move. It somehow seemed important to do it all at once, as if the eagle might escape if I just damaged part of it. The line went through the head, then through one wing, in a curve across the body and out through the tail in a long s-shape.

I stood back and threw down the stick.

"Excellent," said Mr Santos. "The eagle is still free, but

your fear is destroyed. You're all right now, aren't you?"

What could I say when he had taken so much trouble? I said, "Yes," but it wasn't true.

That night the eagle and my fear were in my dreams; and next day when we left the logging camp and walked back through the forest, my fear hung over me like a cloud.

A stone got into my shoe and I knelt down to undo the laces. The others walked on. They didn't know they were leaving me behind and I was embarrassed to call them back. I thought I'd already made enough fuss. I got the stone out of my shoe as quickly as I could and pushed my foot back into it.

And then – it still shocks me when I think of it – something dropped out of the sky like a falling stone. It cut out the sun, so for a moment I was in a tiny pool of night. Something living and warm and heavy thudded into my shoulder and knocked me over. Coarse feathers brushed against my skin, and as I rolled on my back all I could see were great wings.

I lay still, hardly breathing, and I saw the eagle surging upwards again; and I understood why it had swooped – it was carrying a king cobra. I could see the long body and hooded head hanging from its talons. I heard running footsteps and I was aware Mr Santos was beside me; but I couldn't look away from the eagle, rising into the sky.

The thin, dark length of the snake was still twitching, though its head had been crushed. But the thing was – the really extraordinary thing was – it looped from the eagle's claws in a sweeping s-shape, exactly matching the line I had scored through my earth drawing.

Mr Santos pulled me to my feet and he looked really serious. He told me it was as well the eagle wasn't as afraid of me as I was of him, because cobras are deadly.

The others were thumping me on the back and telling me I was a hero. I'm not sure why. I said to Mr Santos, "He saved me. He knocked me away from the snake. It must have been really close. He knocked me out of the way."

Mr Santos said the eagle was only interested in catching a meal. And I knew that, of course I knew that – and I don't think I was ever able to explain properly how I felt.

But the thing I had really feared – the eagle, the spirit of the forest, swooping out of the sky onto me – had happened. He had been so close, I could smell him, feel his warmth, sense his weight; and yet I was all right. He had dropped down onto me and the impact had rolled me clear of the snake. My fear had come real, the worst had happened; and it was all right – I wasn't afraid any more."

CHAPTER ELEVEN

Lee had a plan as detailed as a military manoeuvre.

All mobiles were checked and found to be working. Then each number was keyed into the memory of all the others, so that hitting a single key would automatically dial the phone of choice. As the camera operators, Lee and Jake were 1 and 2. The others, at random, were Hannah on 3, Jenny 4 and Miguel 5. Anya, whose sound mike would be plugged into one of the cameras, would be with one of the camera operators and didn't need to be on the list. All mobiles were set to vibrate, not ring.

Each of them, said Lee, would watch from sites he had already chosen. They would walk together round the five sites while he pointed them out, and then go to their positions.

Anyone who saw or heard the creature could alert the others, whose mobile display would show who was calling. "Call only the cameras," said Lee.

"What about the rest of us?" said Hannah.

"I am sorry," said Lee. "But one person moving towards the animal is likely to send it into hiding. Five would be certain to."

"Then why have we all put our numbers in?" said Jenny.

"So that Jake and I know who is calling and where to go," said Lee. "No one need speak."

As they followed him around the edge of the wood to the far side, where the outermost trees touched the sheep field, they realized it was not as large as they had thought. Viewed from the camp at the tarn's edge, the heights of the pines and other conifers, and the darkness trapped between their trunks, made it seem like a forest. In fact, though, it was no more than half a mile across.

"Jake," said Lee, "this will be your position. Find yourself a place at the edge of the trees here, where you are hidden but have a view of the field, in case it attempts to take another lamb."

Jake wasn't listening and neither was anyone else. They were all staring at the field.

It sloped away downwards to a narrow stream and then up on the other side. Over to the left there was a belt of trees and the roof of the farmhouse could just be seen, half-hidden in a hollow far away to the right.

But it was the sheep they were looking at.

Presumably still nervous after the killing of the ewe – and more recently the lamb – they were not scattered but close together, near the stream, some lying down, a few still cropping the grass. At the edge of the flock, two extraordinary creatures stood close together, ears up, looking across at them warily.

"Llamas!" said Jake.

"The farmer's 'heavies'," said Lee

"And definitely not armed," said Anya.

"They will quickly regard themselves as part of the flock," said Lee, "and will defend it from predators."

"Even a predator strong enough to drag a sheep halfway across a field?" said Jake.

"Foxes certainly, dogs almost certainly," said Lee. "They are strong and brave and can deliver a powerful head-butt. This encounter might be a little different. I am not sure. I don't know."

They headed back through the wood, walking quietly, not talking, in the hope of creating as little disturbance as possible. Silently, Lee indicated his chosen sites. He would keep watch on the creature's larder, where the roast chicken bait lay. That, he thought, was the most likely spot, and he kept Anya with him, in the hope of catching good quality sound. The sheep field, with its live bait, was the second most likely, which was why he wanted Jake on watch there.

He placed Jenny back at the camp, and Miguel and Hannah at two other places within the wood which would give the team maximum coverage.

As soon as they were back at camp, with everybody aware of where everybody else would be, he looked up at the sky, then down at his watch, and said, "One hour until sunset. It is time to take up our posts. This may require all your patience, and more."

"The sky's clear," said Jenny, "and there's a full moon."

"A werewolf moon," said Hannah.

"A hunter's moon," said Lee.

Patience was certainly necessary. It was hard to find a position in which it was possible to sit without fidgeting. Even if they managed that, there were other problems – cramp, crawling insects and a kind of anxious boredom.

Jenny, sitting hidden by the Landrover, with the tarn behind her and the trees in front, felt as if she had been left behind. It was never going to come back here to the camp, she felt sure. One of the others – perhaps even all of them – would solve the mystery without her. She had to fight down the old feelings of irritation and resentment that everyone else seemed about to know things she didn't.

As the darkness steadily grew from below – though the last of the light was still in the sky – Miguel found himself looking up through the pines, half-expecting something to be watching him from above. He had to concentrate on the memory of the relief that had flooded his mind when the eagle had struck him, and not on the sense of foreboding he had felt all those years ago in the Philippines jungle.

As the sky darkened and the moon rose, sending slivers of ethereal light down through the trees, Anya had to work hard to focus on what was really in front of her and not to see pale, luminous ghosts drifting to and fro past the dark trunks. She was ready to record, but with Lee beside her didn't feel the same sense of responsibility as the others. Lee was unlikely to miss anything, and as soon as he began filming she would start recording.

Hannah, increasingly aware that a still, dark wood is never silent, even on a windless night, listened to the soft whisperings and clicks that surrounded her, constantly turning to look behind her. She had no idea if mice and voles and beetles were foraging harmlessly, or if something large was moving carefully closer and closer.

Jake was hearing as many soft, unidentifiable sounds and seeing as many strange effects of the light as the rest of them; but his position at the edge of the wood gave him a longer, wider view, so he was plagued by even more tricks of the light. In particular, he kept staring at the narrow belt of trees running down the side of the field to his left. Two or three times he thought he saw movement there, but he couldn't be sure. It was tempting to keep the camera focussed in that direction; but if he did that he risked missing something moving through the wood to his right, the more likely direction.

Looking to the right along the tree line that formed the border of the wood, he found himself watching a deep patch of shadow on the ground, only about four metres away. Idly, he wondered why he was looking at one shadow when there were so many.

Then it seemed to move. He stared until the place he was staring at lost all reality for him – and then blinked hard to clear his vision. When he looked again the shadow was no longer back between two trees, but slightly in front. He glanced briefly at the moon, wondering if it were possible that it's angle could make a tree throw a shadow in front of it, onto the edge of the field.

And then, as he watched, the shadow inched forwards into the field, in the direction of the flock with its attendant llamas as pale as phantoms in the moonlight.

CHAPTER TWELVE

Clear of the trees, the shadow took shape. It was an animal, definitely an animal. He pressed the first digit on his phone, then raised the camera and began filming.

It edged forward again, well into the field now, all its attention on the flock down by the stream. Then it sat up on its haunches for a better view. In that brief moment Jake understood why Hannah had been unable to describe it. It looked like a cross between a bear and a raccoon, but smaller than a bear and larger than a raccoon, and without the raccoon markings.

As he filmed he was aware first of a sudden movement way beyond the animal, to his right. And then a shot. And half a second later something seemed to come from the left – unless it was a ricochet.

The sheep bolted across the field, the llamas with them, and then stopped in a huddle, surging back and forth, uncertain where the danger was coming from.

At the same time, the animal dropped down onto all fours, ran briefly forwards – then changed its mind, spun round and dodged back towards the wood. But as it ran it seemed to lose its sense of direction. Then it fell, struggled up and headed for the safety of the trees, turning to lick at itself and then limped on until it disappeared into the darkness.

All this was over in a couple of seconds. Lowering the camera to try and follow it, Jake saw a man running towards him across the field from the right and another, moving more slowly, approaching from the trees to the left. So there had been a figure hiding there!

Jake got to his feet, shaken. Next moment Lee was at his side and the others, alerted by the shot, appeared one by one.

"What happened?" said Lee, but before Jake could answer, the running figure was upon them. It was the farmer, out of breath but triumphant.

"You should have warned us you were going to shoot," Jake spat at him. "You could have killed some-one."

The farmer ignored him. "I got it!" he said. "Did you see how it staggered? Got to find it now and finish it off." He punched the air. "Great!" he said. "I thought I missed. I thought the shot went wide."

"Did he kill it?" said Miguel as the farmer crashed off into the undergrowth.

"It seemed wounded," said Jake, shaking his head.

"Come on," said Lee. "He is over-excited. If it goes to ground he won't find it."

"Whatever it is, I don't want to find it just for him to kill," said Jenny.

"It is a hunter's duty to find and dispatch an animal he has wounded," said Lee. "Spread out. Call if you see anything. Now it has been shot there is no longer a need to be quiet."

As the others moved off through the trees, Jake caught at Hannah's arm and held her back. "It definitely seemed wounded," he said, "but the weird thing is he did miss. He nearly got me. Look!"

Hannah looked where he pointed and saw the splintered bullet hole in the pine trunk behind Jake.

"You must have been kneeling down," she said.

"I was."

"But if you'd been standing up..."

"Exactly."

Hannah gave him a quick hug. "That stupid, stupid man," she said. "He knew we were around... And who's that?"

Jake looked behind him. The figure he had seen approaching from the trees to the left was crossing the field towards them, not fast, but with a determined air – a tall, very elderly man struggling to carry some kind of very large box.

"That shot," he said as he reached them. "Was it killed?"

He dumped his burden on the ground and they could see it was an animal cage with a strong mesh door and a carrying handle.

"He missed," said Hannah. She pointed to the wounded pine trunk.

"But it staggered," said Jake. "It acted wounded. Are animals hypochondriacs? Could it have been in shock?"

"Ah," said the man. "Good. That means I got it with the tranquillizer dart. Used to win cups for marksmanship – glad to see I haven't lost the knack."

Instinctively Jake looked down at the man's hands, but he wasn't carrying anything that could have fired a dart.

"Back among the trees there," said the man, guessing. "Couldn't carry it as well as this thing." Unexpectedly he held out his hand. "Marcus," he said. "And you are?"

They introduced themselves briefly.

"I take it you'll help me," said Marcus. "I need to find it before Rob gets a clearer shot."

The sounds of someone stomping to and fro deep in the wood told them where Rob the farmer was. The others, though, were not far away. Jenny, Anya and Miguel were standing together, watching, as Lee, moving slowly and bending low, followed the tracks of the animal, guided mainly by the musky skunk-like scent trail it had left along the ground.

"I can see no blood," he said, puzzled. "But look what I can see. There."

Marcus and Lee produced flashlights, and the double beam lit up a hairy shape lying awkwardly across a tree root. Its broad head was tipped to one side and the dog-like jaws were open, showing the strong teeth Hannah had seen before. The silvery face mask, the only light colour anywhere on the dark brown fur, ran across the eyes, which were closed. Its body was as solid as a badger, though larger. Its legs were short but powerfully built, and at the end of each large foot were five long, curved, sharp claws.

"What *is* it?" said Hannah.

"Neither feral dog nor werewolf," said Lee, "but a strong, fierce, aggressive beast. A formidable opponent."

"Thank you for leaving us out here alone with it," said Jake acidly.

"I did not imagine any of you would attack it or incite it to violence," said Lee mildly. "You are not its prey."

The sound of their voices brought the farmer to the site of what he thought of as his kill, but Jake, still furious about his near miss, was happy to put him right.

"May I suggest," said Marcus, "that we get him into this cage before he wakes up. I think we have an hour or so, but you never can be certain how much of the drug actually went in."

"What *is* it?" said the farmer, watching as Jake and Lee lifted the beast, which was even heavier than it looked, and manoeuvred it into the cage.

"How would you have done this on your own?" Jake panted.

Marcus patted his breast pocket. "Mobile," he said. "As soon as I had it in this state, I was going to ring my son to help me."

"Is it what you thought, Lee?" said Jenny, as the door of the cage was securely fastened.

"Yes. It's a wolverine."

"Definitely not a badger, then!" said Hannah.

"No, but it is a distant relative of the badger, and also of the skunk and the stoat."

"It's got many names," said Marcus, "as well as wolverine. Glutton and skunk bear among them."

"And in Canada it is sometimes known as mountain devil," said Lee. "It is a native of North America and Eurasia, particularly Russia. I have no idea how it came to be here."

"It was released," said Marcus. "There's a large estate about fifty miles from here. About fifty years ago the then owner created a small private zoo. Over the years most of the creatures have died of old age, but there was a certain amount of successful breeding and one or two captives remained. The estate is up for sale and the present owner is clearing out. The few parrots and reptiles were easily found homes, but there were two problems… I don't know if you are aware of this, but there's a Wels catfish in the tarn, which was dumped a couple of years ago. Not something many people want to take on. This wolverine was the second problem. The owner was running out of time, thought it could fend for itself and misguidedly released it."

"I should have guessed it came from there," said the farmer.

"How did you know it was here?" asked Lee.

"Until I retired, I was the local vet. Most animal gossip comes my way. Some of it from you, Rob."

"Why didn't you do something about it sooner?" said Rob belligerently.

"I tried," said Marcus mildly. "I've been out here several times, but tonight was best. Tonight there was a hunter's moon."

The stories of the tarn monster and the beast of the woods came to a close by the light of that moon. Rob went back to his sheep, his heavies and his dogs. He refused to admit he had been irresponsible, but was visibly shaken after Jake had shown him how close the shot had come. The heavily drugged and heavy-breathing wolverine was carried back to Marcus's hatchback and his son was telephoned to make sure he would be on hand to help unload it. It was to be put into one of the strong pens Marcus had built when he was a working vet and boarding dogs whose owners were on holiday. Plans for its future would be made as soon as possible, he said. A zoo was the most likely outcome, though the thought of somehow getting it to Siberia or Canada and releasing it into the wild was very attractive.

The story of the pilot film, *Alien Invaders*, came to an end later in a rented editing suite in London, where all the footage was finally put together and they could see what they'd achieved on a full-size screen for the first time.

Jake's footage of the wolverine as it crept out of the wood, stalking the sheep, was even better than he'd hoped – and there, in the distance but clearly visible, were the two long-necked llamas, ears alert, staring back at it.

"North meets south," said Lee.

"Yup," said Jake. "Canadian mountain devil meets Peruvian llama. Wonder who'd have won that confrontation."

"That is just one of many things," said Lee, "that we will never know."

So much to tell you

John Marsden

Scarred, literally, by her past, she has withdrawn into silence. She speaks to no one. Then, set the task of writing a diary by her English teacher, she finds a way of expressing her thoughts and feelings and of exploring the traumatic events that have caused her distress.

There is so much she has to say…

"A moving chronicle of personal recovery."
The Observer

Australian Book of the Year

e.l. konigsburg

the
outcasts
of
19 schuyler
place

The summer is just beginning, and Margaret is having a miserable time at camp. She's delighted when her beloved, eccentric uncles and their dog, Tartufo, whisk her back to their home at 19 Schuyler Place.

But Margaret soon learns that her uncles need rescuing too. The three giant towers they have spent forty-five years building in their backyard are under threat by the city council. To Margaret, the towers are irreplaceable works of art. They sing of joy, integrity and history ... and Margaret is determined to make sure they always will.

From the incomparable E.L. Konigsburg, twice winner of the prestigious Newbery Medal, comes this rousing story about art and the fierce preservation of individuality.

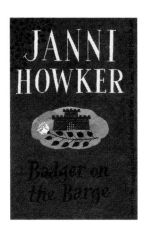

Five award-winning stories, each exploring an often uneasy – but always extraordinary – relationship between young and old. Meet cussed, rebellious Miss Brady, living alone with a badger on her barge; reviled shepherd "Nazi" Reicker; Sally Beck, topiary gardener and one time boy; the sorrowful Egg Man, who cries as he sings; Jakey, a proud, independent fisherman … and the young people whose lives they profoundly affect.

Winner of the International Reading Association Children's Book Award

Shortlisted for the Whitbread Children's Novel Award and the Carnegie Medal